SHIKHANDIN

is the pen name of an Indian writer. She writes fiction and poetry for both adults and children. Her published books, as Shikhandin, include *After Grief* (Red River), *Impetuous Women* (Penguin-Random House India), *Immoderate Men* (Speaking Tiger), and *Vibhuti Cat* (*Duckbill-Penguin-Random House India*). Prior to that a novel and a short story collection were published. Shikhandin's sci-fi story — 'Communal' — was published simultaneously in two anthologies, *A Dying Planet* from Flametree Press and *Avatar* from Future Fiction in January 2020. Her speculative and satirical short story — 'Ruddy Apes and Cannibals' — was one of the most read works at *After Dinner Conversation*, a journal for stories that provoke questions, and is now part of their anthology available from Amazon. Her other fantastika/speculative prose and poetry have been published in *Reckoning, Sybil's Garage, Silver Blade, Enchanted Conversation, Grandpa's Deep Space Diner*, etc. Shikhandin's honours include, runner up George Floyd Short Story Contest 2020 (UK), Pushcart nominee by *Aeolian Harp* (USA) 2019, Pushcart nominee by *Cha: An Asian Literary Journal* (Hong Kong) 2011, Winner Children First Contest curated by Duckbill in association with Parag, an initiative of Tata Trust 2017, First prize Brilliant Flash Fiction Contest 2019 (USA), Runner up Erbacce Poetry Prize (UK) 2019, Winner 35th Moon Prize (Writing in a Woman's Voice: USA), First Runner up The DNA-OoP Short Story Contest 2016 (India), Second Prize India Currents Katha Short Story Contest 2016 (USA), First prize Anam Cara Short Fiction Competition 2012 (Ireland), Long list Bridport Poetry Prize 2006 (UK), Finalist Aesthetica Poetry Contest 2010 (UK). Shikhandin's poetry and prose have been widely published worldwide in journals and anthologies.

Twitter: @Shikhandintweet

The Woman *on the* Red Oxide Floor

Shikhandin

Story Red River

First published in January 2024 by
RED RIVER *Story*

An imprint of
RED RIVER
157/1, Patparganj, New Delhi 110091

(RED RIVER *Story* 3)

ISBN 978-93-92494-49-9

Designed by Dibyajyoti Sarma
Cover art by Shloka Shankar
Cover art Copyright © Shloka Shankar
Typeset in Junicode 11 pt

Printed and bound in India by
Rathna Offset Printers
No 40, Peter's Road,
Royapettah, Chennai 14

Price INR 299 | USD 9.99

For
Abhishek Biswas

Limited edition fiction titles from Red River

Editor's Note

The Woman on the Red Oxide Floor slides along multiple lines of merger and erasure. For the editor, it is exciting to see what this does to the story and its characters. For the publisher, it is challenging to see where and how such a narrative can be placed. This book started with a single tile that held a pattern, but that pattern was not clear, it had not yet found its shape and size and reflections, not yet joined the other tiles that would lay out the complete design. But the faint outlines of that final form peeped out here and there. All that was needed was for the imagination to take hold of that faint promise and allow it to unfurl.

This book is a courageous play of the imagination, untethered, a fantastical leap of faith that must first erase known structures in order to form new patterns. In doing so, the narrative draws in elements of different genres, creating a sense of strangeness that challenges our notions of comfort and discomfort.

The cosmic segues fluidly into the material, human world; a baby is born and finds itself gradually alienated from its sense and memory of an earlier existence, of another cosmos; the insecurities of a mother's world flow into the compulsions of a wife's struggle; the reality of violence creates a fugue that eventually must find its way through the haze to the other side.

Motherhood seems to exist at the cusp of two continuities – the individual and the eternal. If the eternal seems to be a romantic all-encompassing notion, the individual is laced with irony and with that forever-state of being caught between acceptance and defiance.

Mamma, the woman of her imagination is always happy. She must be. She must be happy. She must not have any ambitions other than taking care of Baby Blue. She must live in a nondescript city-town or town-city, where her husband has a job. Her home must be a rented house with a garden and the landlord living upstairs with his wife and inquisitive daughter. She must balance neighbourliness and her boundary for privacy without becoming friendless. She must be that mild, non-threatening provider of food and hospitality to her husband's friends and colleagues and their wives. Mamma's wants must be minimal, because that is the only way a real woman can be happy. Is she real, the woman ponders. Was I real? That me who used to be so unlike the me today. Then again, what does it mean to be real?

The mother-as-an-individual harks back to the woman as a unilaterally gendered entity, established at the very beginning of the story:

And what is lying on the floor is only a woman. Nothing of any importance. Nothing extraordinary. Nothing.

Out of this ordinariness, this nothingness, the character embarks upon a fantastical voyage of discovery, rediscovery, and being. Her thoughts and imagination float away from the material, concrete realities of her immediate experience into the abstract, cosmic largeness of creation.

Somewhere within the deep recesses of the universe or multiverse, there is a stir. Something begins to get displaced. A dream begins to take shape. But neither time nor physical space can contain it. It is happening inside a moment so elastic that it could be as long as a day, a month, a year, a lifetime. Or a second. The blink of an eye.

Worlds are conceived; worlds emerge, merge, fade out, leaving behind one sound, one impression into which the woman melts again and again. The cosmic sound of Om.

The story is about lost hopes and lost worlds, and therefore about loss. But it is also about hope. About dreams dreamt, about reimagining what one has lost, about erasing dystopic melancholy with the anticipation of regrowth, resurgence.

We have only one way ahead: dream future worlds of hope and promise, something different from what we have lived all these centuries, different from the dystopias we have imagined and have begun to live, even outlive, perhaps. Something that is more in touch with inner selves, inner universes, in touch with our stardust not as fantasy but as genesis of all that we are and all that we will ever be. The book holds out the promise of this possibility through its slipstream narrative.

She stares at the sky and the trees below it. The dark shapes of homing birds. White flowers opening their petals to greet the night. Passing clouds form a shape in the darkening sky. The woman looks up and sees another woman there. A young woman with faith in her heart, and a smile on her face. The clouds dissipate. A slow shift of light and air. The image dissolves. Lines of smoke drawn by an invisible and eccentric artist. Silence descends like a celestial feather. She feels forgiven. She feels released. She breathes in a long breath.

*

RED RIVER *Story* hopes to bring to readers stories that are submerged in the rush of those that are more popular, more immediately acceptable, recognisable. *The Woman on the Red Oxide Floor* is one such story. Let its strangeness disconcert you, then ease back, let the music of its inner world waft through your senses. For, in the writer's own words: *This world is nothing but a dream populated by dreamers.*

Sucharita Dutta-Asane

The Woman *on the* Red Oxide Floor

Before the Beginning Began There was the Word
That Word is *OM*
After the Ending Ends There will be the Word
That word is OM
The Hum of The Universe is *OM*

∞

Memory can flash its wings like a butterfly and take away a sliver of your mind, rendering you temporarily insane. All it takes is a moment, and you can go back anywhere in time, revel, or wallow in that state.

Thus, it happens that an afternoon opens its shutters like a window, revealing a woman, prostrate upon the floor.

The woman is young, in her mid-twenties, and sad. She is as sad as one who has experienced death and is yet to recover from its blow. She is lying on the floor, which is made of red oxide, an inviting colour to anyone who has been standing in the hot sun outside. The front of her shirt is crumpled under her breast. Her bare midriff is flat on the floor, skin on cold cement. The right side of her face is also flat on the floor. Her eyes trail the expanse of the red, cool and soothing surface around her. She draws in air cooled by the floor through her nostrils, and it feels like nectar down her throat. The walls of the room are smooth and lime-washed. To the casual observer it's a serene afternoon. And what is lying on the floor is only a woman. Nothing of any importance. Nothing extraordinary. Nothing.

She is not weeping, at least there are no visible tears. Her cheeks are dry. From time to time she convulses, trembles like one having a seizure. Her arms outstretched, she claws the hard red surface. Her nails make a scratchy sound, which would normally have set her teeth on edge, but now her senses are elsewhere. Her breath comes out in gusts and gasps. She feels acutely bereft. The way a mother would when her baby is dead. But her baby is not dead. She has merely sent him away to his grandparents' home. She did it herself. Yes, she did. Though, at this time, she is unclear in her head about the how and why.

They are to be parted for only a few days. But she has never been separated from her baby before. Ever. She had no idea how it would turn out — she and her baby kept apart. She does not know how she agreed to it. But she did. At that time, it had seemed like a good idea. A tunnel of relief had dug itself in her mind at the notion of a few baby-less days. Everyone had said as much, including her husband. She had gone along with it, believing she was not efficient enough, and the baby was better off with her parents-in-law. The relief had filled up again, too soon, leaving behind a trail of unsettled feelings like heaps of loosened soil.

The woman has no family to call her own, so there was no one to advise her. She has often felt inadequate even though she rustles up full course meals for her husband every day, and the weekly dinner guests, keeps a spick and span house and takes care of her baby all by herself. She is always unsure. And now, she lies here, prostrate upon the floor of her bedroom, having returned from the city which is a few hours train journey from the town where her husband is posted, and where she has set up her nest. One piece of solid furniture, one utensil, one appliance, and one item of soft furnishing at a time. There are some makeshift bits too. Items of everyday use that she and her husband put together, like the plywood tea chests they painted over to use as side tables and lamp stands. Her dining table made from two smaller tables, the shoe rack from bricks and a couple of wooden planks. She has stitched half curtains from old saris and stuffed old clothes into quilted fabric pieces in a variety of shapes to make cushions. She has hand-knotted coconut fibre ropes to make mats for her front door and the bathrooms. She is nimble with her fingers. But once upon a time, not too long ago, she used to go to office in smartly tailored clothes. She was a rising star then, according to her ex-boss.

She remains lolling on the floor, letting the emptiness gut her. Her life feels like a gourd from which all the good edible portions have been scooped out. Her womb feels as if it has emptied itself so efficiently that it can never be full again. The notion grips her then, that perhaps her baby has left her forever, and her eyes fly open at the thought, which has begun to unhinge itself like a python's maw, ready to swallow her sanity. Her pain is so vivid and alive that it is like a powerful energy, shaking something beyond the dimensions known to mankind.

She opens her lips, her breath touching the cool of the floor, letting a drop of saliva trickle down. She inhales as she closes her mouth. A word forms around her lips. It is an ancient word. It is a word that could well have been the very first utterance of a word from the mouth of a human.

'*Om*,' she whispers. '*Om. Om. Om.*'

The syllables hum and thrum, pulsating through her being. A low buzz tunnels its way into her ears, shutting out any sound from the physical world. She moves her tongue, and tries to say the words that come after *Om*, the Gayatri Mantra, but something numbs her. Her body soaks in the vibration of the word. Her mind, heart and mouth remain on *Om*, even though she is unable to utter it aloud again.

Somewhere within the deep recesses of the universe or multiverse, there is a stir. Something begins to get displaced. A dream begins to take shape. But neither time nor physical space can contain it. It is happening inside a moment so elastic that it could be as long as a day, a month, a year, a lifetime. Or a second. The blink of an eye.

When she closes her eyes on *Om*, the woman feels it throbbing on the inside of her wrist, at the dimple of her clavicles, her ankles, near the arch of her feet, everywhere in fact, where a big vein ferries life sustaining blood. She sees neither the black sheet of a starless night nor the orange halo that eyelids bring to the closed eye. In the void there is peace. In the physical space her body inhabits — on the ground floor of a double-storeyed house with a garden, in a quietly humming town deep in the pocket of an ancient land cradled in the third planet from a star we call the Sun — the air shifts to let in a cooler draft. Dusk slinks in and starts licking up the light from the sky's face. But time has formed a cyst around her. It is as if she is no different from a foetus inside a woman's body. Even as she feels the emptiness of her womb, she fills up a void with her mind.

It is true. The woman has a wild imagination. It is a beast

with a will and cunning of its own, and she cannot control it. It often takes her galloping down unfamiliar terrain. Sometimes leaving her there abruptly, to find her way back, stumbling and in agony or ecstasy. She has often lost hours in a good day. Hours she could have put to good use, made something of herself, instead of going around in circles, exploring the labyrinths of her febrile imagination.

She is a housewife. She goes about her household chores with care, sometimes with too much care. She appears immersed in her role as wife, mother, daughter-in-law, and all the other roles an ordinary middle-class woman is supposed to take up. She believes this to be just a part of who she is. She does not realise that this is her status and this is how the world sees her. Everyone around her — her husband, her in-laws, her few relatives, her husband's colleagues, her landlord and his family, the neighbours, and acquaintances in the town where she is living now, where her husband has found a job — know her to be a housewife. She does not get it. She is bewildered and very often hurt when they do not take her seriously. When they trivialise her opinions.

As she goes about her chores, she imagines making friends with important people, famous thinkers, philosophers, movie stars and princesses. She has lively conversations with them. They eat and drink with her as they talk. They respond gravely or laugh with genuine warmth when she speaks. Her dining table is a pair of conjoined square folding tables made from iron pipes and a sheet of tin, the kind used at public gatherings and cheap tea shops. Her husband tied the legs together to form a single rectangular table, which she covered with a colourful plastic tablecloth. It is a little wobbly, and can seat six uncomfortably. The chairs are matching folding ones. She got a tailor to stitch cotton seats and backrest covers. Her 'guests' gather at this very table, populating her mornings and afternoons, but disappearing before dusk, when her husband is back home.

The distance from her dining room to the kitchen has often been a ramp or short flight of stairs leading to a podium where she has either stood to give a fiery speech or receive some recognition or the other. All the while the rice has boiled, or the fish has fried or her baby has rocked, and the sunlight has poured down in mellow gold bars on the red oxide floors of her rented home.

Today, however, her hitherto loyal sun has turned his back on her. There are no visitors, and no food is being cooked in her kitchen. Today she is a woman lying on the floor, the cold of the ground seeping upwards, through her skin into her womb and her heart. Today her soul has lifted its face up towards the space where blinding light throws up the shadows in stark relief, listening to the primal stories as they fall earthwards. Today her soul sees the shape of a particular dream as it descends. But her soul is strongly bound to her body. It does not remember what befell before it began dreaming itself. It does not see the oneness of the stories, the eternal cycle. And the prone woman only dimly understands what she is now experiencing. Nevertheless, a sense of dread and foreboding washes over her. In the receding light she raises her head to catch a glimpse of herself in the narrow mirror on the door of the steel almirah in her bedroom. This is the most expensive item of furniture she possesses, and she keeps the metal surfaces of the almirah and the mirror spotless. Her angle is wrong now, and she can only see a partial reflection. An older woman's gaunt face framed by stylishly coiffed grey hair stares back at her. The background, partly visible, shows up not a red oxide floor but something expensive, the corner of a carved rosewood bed, a silk duvet's trailing tassels. Her heart misses a beat. She shuts her eyes to the apparition, whose face is so strangely familiar. When she opens them again, the setting sun's light has crept out of the mirror. She feels the pull of her own ordinary life, but it's a feeble tug.

She has waded too far into the dream.

0

A moment of consciousness ago — it could be a few hours or days, months, years or even a millennium, for time is nothing but a human invention — Baby Blue was sifting through the light between galaxies, just as a toddler on a beach sifts through sand, watching the sparkle with innocent delight. Baby Blue hummed the songs he had picked up from the magnetic fields of galaxies, stars, and planets. He coasted from one star system to the next. Not alone. Never alone. The multiverse is populated with others like him, and, regardless of their genetic and molecular make-up, they are all children of the stars. Sometimes, a tender hand patted his bottom and sent him on his way to the world within worlds, where he would lay down to rest, without any dream to disturb him.

Now Baby Blue feels a sudden jerk. As if an unseen hand has parted the fabric of his universe. He feels eyes boring down on him. He shivers as he turns. He freezes in shock. The starer is not from his realm at all. She is a creature of flesh and blood. She is a living human. Yet, she appears to be so large that she seems to have taken up a chunk of the ether, and her silhouette has obliterated entire star systems from view. Her face, with their intent eyes on him, is like a screen in the shape of a human head, hiding galaxies of swirling stars.

Who is she? Why is she here? Alarm grips him. He tears his sight away from the woman and focusses on '*Om*,' the word that has been resonating since eternity throughout the multiverse and all dimensions.

Almost immediately Baby Blue feels a different touch, but from familiar hands. Suspicion glides through him. The hands lift him up quickly, and he finds himself cradled between two sets of fingers and a pair of palms, interlinked to form a crib. He is being rocked to sleep. This will be a sleep of dreams, but he does not want this sleep.

He can feel the woman staring. He is afraid that once

he enters the dream, she will find her way into it, and he does not want that. The world, his world, is all around him now, full of light and joy. In his world there is no hunger, no pain, no bereavement, no betrayal, no deceit, no meanness, no envy, no violence, no tears, no heartbreak.

Why do these new words trickle into him as the dream hovers above him? Where is he going in his sleep? He does not know. He does not want to know. Right now, the only comfort is the pair of hands cradling him. The sensation is like floating inside a lotus, with its petals wrapped around him. He feels safe, though unwilling to fall asleep. He murmurs his complaint as he fights the sleep; he fights the voice that slides as smooth and as soft as a newly unfurled lotus petal.

I do not want this sleep of dreams, he says to the voice. It is taking me away from you. Why is it necessary? Why must I go through with it? And who is that looking on? Who? Who? Who?

Never mind the who. Focus on the why, comes the reply. Why are stars born and why do they die? Do they really die? Or change into something else? Galaxies expand and contract. It is cyclical. It is not necessarily a rule. If you will yourself not to sleep like a dreamer, you will not. Oh, my child who does not wish to sleep, you do not wish to descend into the world of illusion that I am weaving now, at this very moment. I too am loath to tear you away from this, this most intangible, yet most eternal and true of all bliss. But sleep you must. Dream you must, even for a little while. Even for a fleeting span of time, you must let yourself be bound to time, which is a human folly. But you will understand it once you are dreaming. You will fling yourself back into my arms once the dream is over. Your tears will be mine, even in your dream. Even though you will not know it. Come my restless little one. It is time to lay you down and let the dream begin.

Baby Blue whimpers. He struggles and lies still, trusting, believing, but restless nevertheless. His restlessness comes from a feeling of being watched. The watcher is far beyond his line of vision. The watcher is not of his vast world, though certainly a part of it. The watcher is watching and listening from somewhere small, and deep. A place within the recesses of the vastness of Baby Blue's world. What was said to him just now? The world of illusions that is being woven, now, even as he struggles against it. He turns to the voice and hears the soothing words lulling him again.

Do not be afraid, my child, for I hold you still. You will see my hand moving, but as a blur. You will hear my voice and it will be less than a whisper. And you will laugh, though with little understanding. Already I can feel your finger that was so firmly clasped in mine beginning to relax its hold. Your eyes are now awaking to the dream. Now you know that there is joy here too. A tangible, temporary joy that ends in pain. But this was not always so. My love never wavers. But so often the dreamers go their own way. They push my thought aside, like an unnecessary illusion. They believe in their dream too much. In their dreams they forget. I let them. For I know they will remember again. Then they will return and weep in my arms, and be at peace again. Go now, my little one. Draw your own pattern in the dream.

Stranded in this strange afternoon, which grips her in the stranglehold of incomprehensible alarm, the woman hears and sees the story unfurl. The voice fades. She begins to see the march of characters and events in the story from behind her closed eyes. Much of it is part of a familiar story, one that she had forgotten. Now lulled by the uncanny stillness, she lets go, and plunges into Baby Blue's world.

'*Om*,' she whispers without even being conscious, as if the word is a panacea for all her aches and pains. '*Om Om Ommmm*.'

Her nerves vibrate. Her cells vibrate with the resonance of the word. She is neither dead nor alive. Her heart feels like a cupped hand now, receiving the manna of dream.

Baby Blue tries to rouse himself. But the sleep is a sweet sensation, and he drifts into it, lets himself be pulled in, the way an errant comet would when it meets the event horizon of a black hole. He feels himself falling and falling. And then he reaches a point of no return, a crossroad. Time splits into a pause. Baby Blue feels the jostle of others like him, waiting for their turn.

He stirs sleepily when his turn comes. The dream weaves its web around him. And Baby Blue descends further. A feather shed by a celestial bird in its endless flight, he wafts down. A slant of soft summer rain, he courses down. A soft breath of life, he entwines a man and a woman together, ripens their desire, until it spills over. A sunbeam through the crack of a roof; a spasm through flesh moist with love; a murmur in the tender, shadowy world of a woman's womb; this is the beginning of the beginning of life on Earth for Baby Blue Bottom.

I

Mamma sighs with a longing she has never felt before. She rests her head on her husband's chest. Baba strokes her cheek, her virgin breasts. Together they breathe. Together they fall asleep. Today is a Sunday, and this is their post lazy Sunday lunch hour of tenderness and siesta. The afternoon murmurs around them, like a flock of pigeons in a far courtyard. Mamma feels her eyes droop, but suddenly she is awake again.

Mamma's eyes fly open.

A watchful silence shrouds her.

Instinctively, she gathers the bedclothes around her body. Her eyes dart here and there. The bedroom surrounding her is serene, ordinary, sparse. It is the home of a pair of people who have recently joined their lives together. It does not have too many things in it. She looks at the curtains she had put up a few days ago. They hang with barely a flutter. The windows are shut tight. The door is closed. The fan is a slow whirr. Then why does she have this disconcerting sensation of being spied upon? Why does she sense a presence? She turns her face towards baba. He is snoring lightly. She burrows into his chest where the hair curls and nudges her face into the comfort of his skin and the faint scent of soap.

*

Blue Bottom floats in a miniature cosmos, in fluids that protect and nurture him. But soon his sleep is disturbed. New tremors come rippling in, as if his universe is being torn asunder.

A great gush washes him towards a tunnel fast approaching. He is propelled towards light. His newfound olfactory senses balk at the unknown gases rushing up at him, sucking him into a colder, wider, brighter world, one he cannot trust.

Shell shocked, he cries out with his newfound voice. Someone who seems to be speaking from a faraway place speaks soft words of comfort, but he is not comforted. The speaker does not belong here, does not even exist here. If he was more conscious of himself and his surroundings, Baby Blue would have questioned the speaker. Instead, he slithers on cold metal, because gloved hands have pulled him out and put him there. Those hands, with their unfriendly smell of rubber and blood slap his bottom, turning it blue. Baby Blue has no prior knowledge of metal or rubber or blood. Everything is a first-time experience for his new born body. Everything is strange and hostile. With his quickening senses, he hears and smells the strange and blurry world surrounding him. Blue kicks and thrashes. Voices from this new world, which is his world now, rise and fall around him.

When Blue awakens from his baby slumber, he finds himself submerged in shadows. For a few seconds he believes himself to be in the warmth of the womb. But the cold air sluicing his little lungs reminds him that he is not. His brow puckers as a memory comes floating down.

His eyes that seem unfocussed to his mamma and baba, are looking beyond the three dimensions. He can still see the world he had come from, where his playmates were, and still are, frolicking among the galaxies, the hand that had rocked him into this sleep of dreams is rocking the others. Instinct tells Blue Bottom that he will be able to look at and not through the shadows and smudges that bring so many kinds of sounds and smells with them. Once that happens, he will no longer be able to see all that lies outside the three dimensions of his present world. His old world will become hazier as the days go by. In this world, time obeys a man-made machine called the clock. Everything is not routine though. There is something here that is out of the ordinary, and Baby Blue can sense it like a breath on the nape of his neck.

A new sensation sends spasms through him. This is his second experience with pain. This pain is more basic to his flesh and fleshly needs. Mamma's exhausted hand reaches for the bell. The nurse tucks Blue into her inexperienced arms. Brusquely unbuttons her nightdress. Gently, but firmly positions Blue's mouth directly below her swollen nipples. His nose twitches, and his eyes close with contentment. He suckles. Mamma wipes the milk dribbling off his chin. She rocks him ever so gently, afraid because he is so fragile.

Baby Blue sleeps, and in his sleep, he returns to the hands that cradled him. In his earthly sleep, Blue returns to the world from where he has come. His eyes are yet to receive clear vision, and earth's light has not yet poured into his pupils. They are still foggy. His eyelids droop over them and instantly transport him back. Mamma and baba watch his face twitch, his baby lips stretch into a smile sometimes, or crumple into an unuttered sob.

Mamma has a steady stream of visitors at the hospital. Relatives and friends, and even old servants who are like family members, have come to celebrate the birth and stake their claim over the new born. They whisper that an infant being a pure being is still able to converse with God. They consider him God. He is a little Gopala, baby Krishna. And sometimes he is the blue-throated God, Shiva, in his baby form.

To the elders, Blue is divine and will remain so until he begins to walk firmly and talk clearly. The old maid, who mamma does not like, keeps trying to take Blue into her lap, whispering prayers and singing bhajans. Mamma only wants to be allowed her maternal rights. She is discomfited by the constant reminder that her child is a divine being. She can feel her maternal authority only when he suckles. She feels soothed when he latches. Her pain eases. At times she falls asleep, and when she does, her dreams intertwine with that of Blue's. She sees wonderous things together with him, his hand clasped in hers. She remembers nothing when she awakens. Nothing at all. Except the disquieting thought that in her shared dream with Baby Blue, there had been a third presence.

The woman is beginning to enjoy herself now. The desolation she had felt earlier is peeling away layer by layer. Her curiosity piqued, she wants to learn more and more about Baby Blue's new life and especially his mamma. She sighs as she straightens herself, stretching a little. Mamma has a familiar face, like someone she knows but cannot place. She could have passed her by at the grocery store or bumped into her at a cinema hall or park or even a friend's house. It is not merely that. Her life seems familiar as well, a disconcerting and half-remembered familiarity.

The woman settles herself into a more comfortable position, and lets the story expand around her. For once she feels greater control. This feeling that she has a hold over the narrative and the actors, that she is an empowered entity in that world flows over her like the vibrations of an ululation. Her body loosens as she swims deeper into their world.

She watches the sleeping woman, Baby Blue's mamma, on her hospital bed. Her nightie is of a cheap variety. The kind one would buy from kiosks lining the footpaths of a street full of swanky shops, the kind she herself had once bought. The vermillion in the parting of her hair is a bit faded. The woman knows it will be refreshed before mamma is released from the hospital. Mamma is too traditional to risk snide remarks from the gaggle of relatives awaiting her and Baby Blue at home. The woman smirks as she makes this observation. She no longer anoints the parting of her hair with vermillion.

There is something fragile and serene about mamma in her iron hospital bed and Baby Blue in his iron crib. The room is a soft white and sea green medley of walls and bedclothes. Outside the curtainless window, an unknown bird is calling. The sun bright sky dips into the horizon curlicued by trees and buildings. The woman peers into this world. Inquisitive. Keenly interested in the smallest detail.

Mamma's eyes fly open at the intensity of the woman's stare. Their eyes lock for an instant or two. Mamma's scream is clamped shut by her own hand.

The woman on the other side is shocked as well. What has she just seen? Did she really make eye-contact?

Mamma shuts her eyes and opens them again. Her heart hammers against her ribcage. She is completely awake by now. She looks around her room. She wills herself to see the open window and the sky where she had seen the apparition. Brilliant blue meets her gaze. The houses and trees hum softly in the afternoon. She turns to her baby. She slides towards his little body in the crib. She bends her head to smell his slightly sour baby smell. And then she falls back on her bed. Her post pregnancy-loosened body shakes with a terror that she has never known before.

When Blue awakens, his tender new body flinches. The light keeps changing. As do the sensations of touch and smell. His nappy is changed and a fresh cloth swaddles him again. And again, and again. His new and inexperienced ears pick up the different sounds around him. The visions from his dreaming state melt away in the bright sunlight. His senses struggle to understand the physical world around him. After a while, he recognises, much like a puppy or a lamb, that there is a pattern in which he lives. A routine is followed in which he is fed, and the smell of milk-swollen breasts is soon comfortingly familiar.

A few days later, his routine suddenly changes, even as he remains in mamma's arms, after being wrapped in a fresh cloth, like a snug bug, with only his right arm free.

Blue turns his head this way and that way. He is held tightly in Mamma's arms. They are moving fast. The smells change fast. But the sound, a strange buzzing and droning, does not change at all. His body does not move. Mamma's body does not move. They are inside something. That thing is moving. And they are moving with it. Sometimes Blue feels a jerk. Mamma's grip feels tighter then. He remembers a similar jerk. And the terror that came with it. He tries to remember clearly, puckering up his brow. But the memory eludes him, like an eel among the reeds.

The air rushes past Blue. Joyous, little bubbles of life fly past him. He knows what they are. They are dreams yet to be dreamed, as he once was. They are descending, as he had descended. The songs of their joy caress Blue Bottom like old familiar friends. He believes he is flying too, the sensation is similar. The flying slows to a gentle rocking sensation. Then it stops. He feels a slight jolt. His heartbeat quickens and subsides almost immediately. There is a soft yet strong hand supporting his fragile neck. Blue Bottom looks up. His vision blurs into the material world around him. He cannot see clearly, but he can feel it. He has arrived somewhere.

'Well, mother and child are safely home,' says baba as he helps mamma into the house. 'Never have I driven such a VIP, before!' He jokes and beams at all the grandparents, aunts, uncles, and friends, who have assembled to welcome this precious addition into the family.

Conch shells blow and the ululation of a joyous and auspicious occasion ripples through the air. The warmth from the five flames of the pancha pradeep rests on Baby Blue's forehead like a divine tilak. The women ululate and laugh. From the depths of the house Blue hears an old man chanting the Mahamrityunjay mantra. The reverberating air flows towards him like a divine wave. He senses rather than hears the different notes of love sung at different octaves. The chanting draws him in with a sense of wellbeing.

There is hubbub all around. But mamma's touch and smell envelop Baby Blue in a comforting blanket. He sticks his small mouth into his only source of food and drink. He suckles until his eyes close and his mouth falls away from mamma's breast. As Blue drifts into slumber again, he slips back into a world he used to know well, but a fog seems to be descending now, growing thicker day by day. The sounds which were clear as crystal bells are now increasingly muffled. The colours more muted. The touch, oh the touch of his mates among the stars, they are as fragile as the skins of bubbles, bursting with mere breath. The reality he knew is becoming more and more dreamlike with each passing day.

Time flows, turning the world bright and then dark. Time divides into compartments along the way. Blue begins to recognize each compartment. He does different things in each. He is always in motion. His body is always in a state of expansion. A month passes. His eyes gain clarity of vision. His neck begins to firm up. Another month passes, and he feels stronger, more aware. He recognizes mamma and baba and some of the grandparents and an old maid who keeps returning, again and again, holding him, singing to him, rocking him, sometimes massaging him with oil, and sometimes holding him carefully in a tub full of warm water, that reminds him, increasingly vaguely, of a warm safe place full of nourishing fluid that he had been forced to abandon.

A sunbeam falls on Blue, a feather touch of warmth suffused with rain. He lifts his nose higher, drawing in the sunlight. A familiar lullaby, sung softly in a familiar voice, caresses him from the tips of his twiddling toes to the wisps of downy hair on his forehead. Blue looks up. He can make out a familiar shape and a familiar smell. He feels secure. He gurgles, throws his legs up. It feels good. He concentrates on his stomach to push. His bottom feels sticky and warm after he has pushed. But mamma's hands are always there to make him feel cool and dry again.

Mamma is talking to him now. Blue gurgles as he listens. Then baba's voice joins in. He likes it. He likes the shape and the smell that come with it. Altogether they bring messages of a wider world, one that exists outside this room. To Baby Blue, there is a sense of adventure in baba's presence. He is getting used to baba's hands that are harder, and a bit clumsy at times. Blue finds it funny. Mamma's voice does not sound funny when baba is clumsy. And Blue almost always finds himself back in mamma's arms.

Mamma puts Blue on a perambulator, which to him feels like a moving bed. He likes being in it. Mamma wheels him around the house. She does her work and sings or talks to him at the same time. Blue likes watching the changing scenery. Everything feels like an adventure. Every day brings him something new.

Days pass along with their unchanging routine. Baby Blue's gurgles become louder. His kicking legs get stronger. His neck feels firm enough to hold up his head forever. His eyes open to the brilliance of the expanding world around him. He can roll over on his stomach. He can lift his head up while on his stomach. He can remain propped up against pillows without toppling sideways. He can recognise his possessions, including mamma and baba.

Tears are rolling down the woman's cheeks. But these are not tears of sorrow. They express a singular emotion, one that is a medley of various feelings. But not, definitely not, sorrow. She is watching Baby Blue grow, and that makes her think of her own baby. It is like she is reliving her own experiences. If she could, she would reach over to kiss Baby Blue.

Happy. Happy. Happy. Mamma, the woman of her imagination is always happy. She must be. She must be happy. She must not have any ambitions other than taking care of Baby Blue. She must live in a nondescript city-town or town-city, where her husband has a job. Her home must be a rented house with a garden and the landlord living upstairs with his wife and inquisitive daughter. She must balance neighbourliness and her boundary for privacy without becoming friendless. She must be that mild, non-threatening provider of food and hospitality to her husband's friends and colleagues and their wives. Mamma's wants must be minimal, because that is the only way a real woman can be happy. Is she real, the woman ponders. Was I real? That me who used to be so unlike the me today. Then again, what does it mean to be real?

Baby Blue looks at the pram. He kicks his legs to attract attention. He lets loose his mouth and a cheerful bawl rolls out. He has announced his presence. Mamma comes running in.

'Yeth. Yeth Yeth. Mamma knows what baby wants. Baby wants bye-bye. No?'

Mamma always speaks in this special language with him. Blue knows Mamma made this language only for him. She does not speak like this with anybody else. Not even with Baba. She speaks with Baba in another special language. Not always, but sometimes, when they are alone, and they think he is asleep.

Blue also has his own language. He tries to teach it to both Mamma and Baba, but they are not so quick. Mamma is quicker than Baba. She is also more presumptuous than he, deciding that Blue wants something when he has not asked for it at all. She thinks Blue only talks or cries when he needs something, like changing his nappy. But Blue likes to talk because he wants to talk about the things he has seen, heard, and felt. When his talk comes out like a cry it is because he has sad things to say. Like the shadow he had once seen.

Blue still sees lights and shadows, unlike his parents. These lights and shadows are not of their physical world. Blue, however, no longer recognises them for what they are. He can only feel the emotion they bring. He can feel love, and he has a vague idea about fear, what it is and how it comes. The shadows make him fearful. They feel like a threat to his little fleshly body. When he tries to communicate his feelings to his parents, they fuss over him, but they never understand. They try everything from checking his nappy, to giving him a feed he does not want, to rocking him to-and-fro, to holding him close to their warm bodies and beating hearts. The last helps, always.

Now mamma gets busy over Blue's wardrobe. She likes fussing over his clothes. She puts one set of clothes on him, changes her mind and takes it off. She tries another set, and then another. Blue enjoys the fuss. Sometimes he is impatient for his ride, and bawls. Mamma always picks him up, and walks around the house when he does that.

Blue gets his ride outside the house once every day. When the sun dips low on the other side of the sky. The ceiling recedes and becomes a vast blue dome, reaching unreachable heights. The blue changes, lightening and darkening in cycles. He feels secure beneath the dome, as if it is responsible for containing this reality to earth. But what lies beyond? The question nudges him like a distant bird's call. It reminds him hazily of something he used to know intimately.

His bright baby eyes watch the birds swooping in perfect unison. They follow the ponderous flight of a fruit bat. Mamma always stops and bends protectively over his pram when the fruit bat dips low. The gravel below the pram makes a scrunching noise. The pram wobbles a little now and then. When that happens, mamma checks to see whether his bones are intact. All of a sudden, the scent of flowers surrounds them, and the pram seems to roll over a soft, sweet-smelling carpet. Mamma finds a friend to gossip with. Blue does not mind. The gossip usually centres round him. Blue honours mamma's friend by curling his hand around her finger. The friend is ecstatic. Blue watches a bee zooming in. He hears a shriek. And, mamma, friend and Blue in his pram zoom off to another part of the park.

He gets a chance to enjoy the adventure again in the form of a story, when baba comes home, and mamma gives him a detailed account of the day. The bee becomes an enormous evil creature, mamma the ever-vigilant saviour, and Blue the baby in distress. The best part of this exercise is baba's reaction, the minute mamma goes off to warm their dinner. Baba picks him up and talks man to man. He also plays man to man, well almost. Now he tells Blue that it is silly to be scared of a little bee. And, if he, baba, had been there he would have snapped up the bee with his palm and crushed it to a paste in his fist.

'Haha,' says mamma sarcastically. She has eavesdropped on this part of the conversation.

Baby Blue's routine continues. The adventures change slightly, but baba never seems to tire of hearing each new version when he comes home every evening. Baby Blue has graduated from a diet of only mother's milk to Cerelac and half a mashed banana once a day. He enjoys his oil massage and the wash in a tub more and more, because he can splash the water with his legs. He smiles at mamma every time he sees her, which is every ten minutes. He gurgles every time he sees baba, which is every twenty minutes in the morning followed by a long absence until the sun dips. When baba returns to Blue's universe, he never seems to leave Blue's side.

Today brings home another dusk, and baba is back. Blue yawns. Mamma runs to get him his mashed banana. Baba feeds it to him. Mamma vanishes into a room that Blue has not yet been into. The house becomes smoky. It begins to smell of a thousand perfumes. A bell rings, and a conch bellows. It is just mamma in her Puja room, ushering in the evening. But Blue Bottom is startled. It reminds him of the echo from a thunderous sound, an angry dance of chaos. He is always startled when mamma blows the conch. Baba holds him close to his breast and murmurs soothing words.

Baba's breast is hard and hairy. Blue likes it. He likes the sound of baba's heart booming below his ear. Baba wipes Blue's banana smeared lips. Blue opens his mouth wide, looking at the spoon. Baba laughs. He tells mamma that Blue's appetite has grown. Mamma looks proud. Blue gets to taste something new almost every day. He likes most of them. The ones he does not like, he lets them dribble off his chin. But that rarely happens. And mamma never repeats a bad taste.

The woman heaves and sighs. Her womb feels empty and deserted. It is no longer a happy receptacle for the story or the dream or the dream-story of Baby Blue Bottom. Now it feels like a bowl full of dry ice. The cold burns her. The smoke asphyxiates her. The weightlessness pulls at the substance of her being. She hears the beat of her own heart like the boom of a cannonball. Her eyes have hardened to the waning afternoon. Time has spun off into another zone.

When was the last time she had sat down before a row of holy idols and recited Sanskrit slokas and mantras? When had she last dressed the Lokkhir Ghot? Called friends and neighbours home to celebrate shottonarayan pujo? These were the practises of her mother and all the aunts and neighbouring aunties of her childhood. She has, over the years, turned away from all these rituals. She had initially kept a rudimentary puja room out of respect for her mother-in-law. But when the relationship soured, she banished her collection of brass gods and pancha pradip and other puja paraphernalia to the bottom drawer of a cupboard full of crockery and miscellaneous things.

The left side of her body has gone to sleep. It takes her a while to straighten her leg, and feel the blood circulate again. She used to be so supple. She has not been aware of the swift passing of the days. Her mind has remained trapped in a bubble, and sometimes she mistakes one day for another. It has been like this for years.

She remembers with grimness in her heart, the day she had found a newspaper on the lower tier of her old double-racked coffee table, a piece of furniture she had bought at a trade fair and had become particularly fond of. Instead of tossing the paper into a tall plastic basket with a lid in which she used to store old newspapers, she had sat down to read it. She had read it from end to end with increasing horror, until her entire body trembled with a nameless grief, and forgetting all about her baby sitting on the floor with his toys scattered around him, she had run out to the balcony. Her heart began to pound, and her eyes could no longer hold back her tears.

She had relived the demolition of the Babri Masjid and the carnage that had taken place the previous month, jolting India and the world. Almost the entire newspaper contained stories and photographs about the violence. The newspaper had lain there for a month, and she had not noticed. When her eyes fell on it that day, she saw the day, but missed the date. She mistook the newspaper to be that day's paper. Horror and shame filled her as she read the reports again. The incidents overlapped and looped around in her mind, forming an endless cycle of violent and heart-breaking scenes. It did not take long for her feverish mind to see them as fresh incidents, a horrifying replay, a jamais vu experience. The images flashed all around her. Her mind felt like it was splintering into violent images.

She had run up and down with the paper in her hand, her mind shrieking, 'Again and again! They did it again. Why? Why this senseless endless cruelty?'

She had sat down at last with the newspaper clasped to her bosom, flopping on the floor near her baby. In an act of desperation, she had pulled him close and buried her face into his baby smell and baby touch. The comfort was meagre this time. When she had first read about the incident, she had given a piece of her mind to the mighty political figures she had deemed to be the culprits, right there in her home. She had fed them shukto and dal, cabbage curry and rice followed by tomato chutney and pappad, and sweet curd. She had been hospitable like a true Hindu, and mindful of their vegetarian palates. And then she had lectured them all, and they had heard her out, and even been sorry for what they had unleashed on the country.

Holding the old paper in her shaking hands, the woman saw that they had not heard her at all. Her fevered imagination mocked her, for they had gone back the very next month and demolished the structure all over again! How foolish she had been to believe in humanity.

Time swings the woman back to her present.

The woman studies the memory. And the memory studies her back. A mocking infinity mirror.

She feels confused and bereft. The world is all wrong. Everything has turned against her. Everything is inside-out. Time is a dark angel sitting at the alcove where her deities are supposed to sit. She is adrift in the vast ocean that time has cast her into, in which there is endless today, an everlasting now. She feels helpless and powerless.

In reality, her life has moved on. She is a more experienced mother now, one who has learnt to negotiate with the humans around her without causing undue disruption to the life she shares with her husband. Her baby goes to nursery school these days. Today he will spend the afternoon with his grandparents, they have their uses after all. It was supposed to be a welcome break for her, the mother. That was what everyone had said, and she had believed them. But it turned out differently. She had failed to contain time.

Like before, sending her baby away was not her decision, not entirely, even though she had said yes. It never is, but she never seems to realise it until her baby leaves her, and the emptiness grips her. And now, once more, her routine feels disrupted. She feels her maternal authority thwarted, and that makes her angry. The threats to her loom, always, always. They poison her peace of mind. She could have entered the adult world knowing her baby is safe, for this one afternoon. She could have read the book she had begun a year and a half ago. Or smoked a cigarette. Or simply enjoyed herself window shopping, and maybe picking up pretty trinkets. She did none of these things. She stayed at home and after sometime, found herself prone on the floor. She is once again smothered by a sense of *jamais vu*, like the time she had come apart with the newspaper report. She has been in this situation before, but she cannot pin it down. The events of the afternoon are nothing special, but it has a disquietingly familiar ring to it. She keeps reaching out but her mind yanks the memory out of her reach each time.

Soon homing birds will begin their din in the trees outside. But she feels no inclination to get up and immerse herself in the ordinary things of her life. The vibrations of OM resonate within her. A portal seems to have opened along the lines of her vision on the floor. Time loops back to the first encounter. Her soul erupts from her physical being and drops into the portal. She begins to follow Baby Blue's progress closely. Baby Blue is hers and yet not hers. Baby Blue's mamma is she herself, and yet not she. No, not at all, how could they be the same? They are two different entities. Baby Blue's mamma is a woman she would never be, even though her love for her own offspring is just as fierce. Maybe all mothers, no matter how different their milieus are, belong to a secret sisterhood, obeying the same shaman.

2

Blue wakes up in what looks and smells like a strange house. Strange people are looking at him. Beyond their shoulders, seemingly from the wall, a familiar woman's face stares at him. Baby Blue has grown used to this extra presence. He has tried to point her out to mamma and even baba, but they did not or could not understand. Mamma, to give her credit, seemed worried, even a little afraid, but she had not been able to see, at least not alongside Baby Blue.

Blue sighs. He gurgles half-heartedly. It is his nature to feel happy the minute he wakes up. But not today. The house feels very crowded. It is full of suitcases, bags and bedding. It is full of noise. Blue feels confused. He bawls as loudly as he can. There is an immediate clamour. He hears mamma's name being called out several times. He hears several voices shouting, 'He's awake. He's awake!'

Mamma comes hurrying in. She takes Blue in her arms. Everybody crowds around them. Everybody wants to pick up Blue. Blue does not like it. He clings to mamma and cries. Mamma soothes him. She tells the people to leave them alone for a while. The men and children among the crowd leave. The women do not.

Mamma feels awkward. Blue wants to put his hands on both her breasts. He wants to look at everybody while he suckles. But mamma keeps him covered with the end of her sari. She keeps pushing his hand away from her other breast. Blue feels disturbed. He is curious about all these laughing, gossiping women. But he also wants complete attention from mamma's breasts.

Blue knows everybody is talking about him. He feels their love surging towards him. But Mamma does not feel relaxed. Her tension makes him tense. He does not know whether to trust all these loving people or not. He decides to find out. He goes from eager arms to eager laps. It is nice for a while. Then he bawls for mamma again, but baba comes to him, instead. That seems good enough for Blue. Good enough until it is time for his next meal.

The next meal never arrives. Blue does not miss it. His stomach is full. He has been eating titbits all day. Mamma tries to nurse him, but even the smell of her milk-swollen breasts does not interest him. Mamma feels upset. She grumbles about it in a whisper to baba. He laughs off her complaints. Blue likes baba's company more today. Mamma is just too tense.

Today is Blue Bottom's annoprashon, his rice eating ceremony. Everybody is making a fuss over Blue. Four women are giving him his bath — two grannies and two aunts. The bath takes a long time. It takes so long that Blue falls asleep. Five more join in to help Blue into his clothes. There are many sets of clothes. All of them are brand new. Each bought by an aunt or uncle or grandma or grandpa. Everybody quarrels over which set he should wear. His thakuma is gazing at him with pride. She waves off the others, and takes charge. Someone cracks a joke. Someone else insists on a particular set of clothes. It is a funny quarrel, with everybody laughing and shouting at the same time. They look happy even though they are quarrelling. Blue feels happy too. He has pooped on the sheets that cover his baby mattress, which is always placed on the big bed he shares with mamma and baba. The smell silences the happy crowd around him for a minute or two.

Thakuma scoops him up, and rushes to the bathroom. She washes him, and dries him with her sari end. When she returns to the bedroom, someone has removed the soiled bedclothes but neither wiped the oilcloth on Blue's bedding, nor replaced the fresh sheets. Thakuma places him on another part of the big bed, and powders him and puts on a fresh set of clothes. Someone suggests she put him on a diaper first, but thakuma does not know how these modern things work. So, she ignores the advice and ties a cloth nappy instead, over which she pulls up a pair of shorts matching the shirt. The shorts have elastic both on the waist and the legs. Blue feels them pinching his soft thighs. He hates this and kicks his legs in annoyance. His eyes turn serious, but nobody notices his change of mood.

Blue starts to get irritated with the new clothes. He bawls to let the whole horde know his displeasure. Mamma hurries into the room, and whisks him away from thakuma's arms. The hubbub dies down immediately. Mamma resolutely takes Blue's clothes off. She strips off the cotton nappy and deftly puts a disposable diaper on him. She brings out a package from the cupboard. The package contains yet another set of new clothes for Blue, but these are pre-washed and rinsed with diluted Dettol water. She puts these on Blue. They feel soft. They smell fresh. And there is a bell hanging from a cord attached to the collar of his suit. Blue likes these new clothes. He gurgles at the sound of the bell, which is the only sound left in that room. Everybody is silent. Baba is making discreet faces at mamma from a corner far away.

It does not take long for things to get noisy again. Lights flash all around Blue. There is too much smoke in the room. It smells like mamma's prayer time, only now the smell is stronger. Too strong for Blue. His eyes start to water and he sneezes several times. He looks around for mamma. She usually rushes to his side when he sneezes once. But today she has disappeared from his line of vision. There is a fire crackling in the room, and a strange man with no shirt on is muttering something. There are banana leaves full of fruits and flowers, and other paraphernalia of a religious ritual.

Blue turns his head to look at the person on whose lap he is seated. It is a strange face, a man's face. Blue is too frightened to cry. His lips tremble. He starts to pee in little squirts into his diaper. Exhausted and distressed, he falls asleep. He sees things inside his little head, things that are dreams but do not behave like proper dreams. They are shadowy, dark, and brooding. They dance to the rhythm of the priest's chanting and burrow into his ears. He feels threatened by their slow dance. Their blurry faces disturb him. Their whispered conferences sound like warnings. He does not understand their language, but their intent seems hostile. He tosses in his sleep. He whimpers. He searches for the voice, but he cannot hear it. He calls and calls, his wail slicing through the firmament. Still the voice remains silent. As if it has been pushed out or put off by the clamour of pious rituals.

When Blue wakes up again, disoriented and thirsty, he finds himself surrounded by strange, eager faces. But mamma and baba are there as well. Besides, he is in another room where there is neither smoke nor the strange shirtless man mumbling into the fire. Now there is a shiny plate before him on the bed. It is full of interesting things. Some are shiny, like the coins and bits of gold. There is also a dot pen, a piece of rope, a colourful book, and a tiepin. Blue understands he must pick up these things, but he is so thirsty, and mamma is so far away.

For what seems to be an eternity, Blue studies his surroundings. His eyes express distress as they scan the room. Mamma, who must have sensed, her maternal instincts being on red alert today, is right beside him again. He reaches for her breast, but she thrusts a feeding bottle between his lips. Blue is angry, but mamma's hand is firm. He suckles on the rubber nipple, and something mildly sweet, milky, and warm trickles into his throat. It soothes his thirst instantly.

There is a lot of talk about the objects on the plate, especially the tiepin, because it is not supposed to be among the things that Blue is supposed to pick up. Blue tries to grab the tiepin. He cannot reach it, and instead finds himself grabbing the book. This generates a lot of conversation. Baba picks him up and twirls him around. Everybody starts arguing. Blue is invited to grab the things on the plate again. And this time he succeeds in grabbing the tiepin.

Blue rides on someone's shoulders to the next. Somebody remarks irrelevantly that a tiepin is not supposed to be there. Blue holds up the tiepin like a trophy. He catches mamma looking at him with a tender-proud look on her face. He wants to go to her but he is not allowed to. He is made to sit on an uncle's lap. He is given a spoon of something that feels sticky and tastes sweet. He likes the taste, and opens his mouth for more. This generates a lot of laughter. Blue passes from lap to lap. Spoons and spoons of payesh pass into his mouth. Blue's stomach begins to churn. He throws up.

Now mamma is the only one who comes forward. Blue is hastily handed over to her. The owner of the stained lap rushes off to clean himself. Mamma takes him to the basin. Tenderly she cleans his mouth, face, and hands. The vomit has hurt Blue's nose. He cries and cries. Baba comes into the bathroom. He helps Mamma take off his soiled clothes. Together they take him to their bedroom, which is quiet and cool. Together they soothe him to sleep.

Everything is still when Blue wakes up for the second time since the festivities around him began. The dipping sun tickles him with its soft red rays. The clamour of the birds outside seems far away, because the glass-paned windows are closed. Blue feels the soft arms of mamma on one side. His legs sink into the soft, but firm belly of baba on the other side. He feels he is inside the egg, only this time the egg is made up of mamma and baba. Mamma stirs. She pats Blue's chest. Baba strokes his hair. Blue tries to part mamma's blouse. Mamma tucks his head between her breasts. Blue latches on, contentedly. Nothing tastes as good to Blue. He wants to suckle forever.

The afternoon flumes into evening. The house regains its noise and bustle, softly at first, and then with increasing energy. The house now has extended itself to the garden. Or so it seems to Baby Blue Bottom. Held in baba's arms, he gazes at the scene as baba ambles around greeting people. Blue looks at the fabric wall to his right, bulging in as if pushed by a giant tummy. He looks to his left and there is another wall exactly like it, doing the same thing. There are lights festooned above from one corner to the other. Long tables with people seated on one side, laughing, talking, eating. Fragrant steam from hot food streams in. Baby Blue sneezes. Baba digs his nose into Baby Blue's cheek. Blue gurgles. Strange people come up to him. They wave gifts wrapped in shiny paper. Baba takes them with one hand and either passes them to someone next to him, or places them at a particular table if he is standing near it. But where is mamma? Blue's eyebrows crease slightly. He whimpers softly. Baba kisses him and points out people who wave or smile or react in one cheerful way or other. But Blue does not want them. His eyes rove the crowd for his mamma.

The man who had chanted many prayers before a fire in the afternoon, which had seemed dead to Baby Blue, because he had felt nothing, seen nothing from his past life in those flames, despite all the pious rituals being enacted, now comes forward and grins at baba with a betelnut stained mouth. The man had droned on and on, while the fire spat and smoked, and Blue was made to sit first on baba's lap and then on the laps of a series of people, beginning with his grandparents, and followed by those he had never seen before. It had unsettled Blue, and he carried that negative feeling within him still. Blue looks at the grinning man and sees blood dripping fangs and bulging greedy eyes. His eyes brim with fear, and he lets out a wail. He cannot be consoled. He hears mamma's voice from a distance, 'give him to me, give him to me.' He hears her hurried steps, but they are not close enough, and it is not she who takes him. He is almost pulled out from baba's arms by thakuma. She clasps him to her breast and walks quickly away. Blue looks tearfully over her shoulder. Mamma is almost stumbling as she hurries, the plea in her voice loud enough for several people near them to hear. But Blue's thakuma hurries forward as if she has heard nothing.

When Blue is finally returned to mamma, the crowd has thinned and the hubbub has grown quieter. Mamma takes him away to her bedroom, and gives him her breast. She gently removes the new clothes from his body, as he murmurs into her nipple, his small hands digging into her flesh. She changes him as weariness seeps into his body. She whispers soothingly to him. But it is not her voice that he hears as his eyes begin to close. It is the other, as soft as breath and as regular as a beating heart. The voice is telling him that he is never alone, even when no one is with him. The voice tells him that the pain and fear, the vibes of hostility that he can sense even when they are not directed at him, are as fragile as flesh and bone.

3

Baby Blue Bottom. Chubby and soft, dimpled and double-toothed at eight-months, sits on the red oxide floor with his toys scattered around him. It is late afternoon. The sun's muted orange light seeps through the drawn curtains. Mamma has fallen asleep on the floor, tired out from her endless chores around the house and from baby-sitting the adamantly sleepless Blue Bottom.

He looks at her, a mischievous light in his eyes, and squeezes the blue rubber baby Krishna that someone had gifted him at his annoprashon. The doll has a cheerful indigo blue face and bright pink lips upturned to form an eternal smile. A painted peacock feather nestles on his head which is made of moulded rubber and coloured black to represent hair. Baby Blue glances at mamma and then at the wall.

The wall dissolves beneath his gaze to reveal another room with a red oxide floor, with a woman lying on it in a foetal position. But that woman is not sleeping like mamma. She is looking straight at them. Her unsmiling face is focussed on them as if they are in a movie that she is watching all by herself. Intrigued, Baby Blue crawls towards the woman, and in that instant, mamma wakes up with a start.

Mamma sits up and looks around her in bewilderment. She sees Blue near the wall. Her eyes widen with fear. She cannot see anything other than the pale lime washed wall, but she feels devoured by a pair of eyes, both she and her baby. Her hands fly involuntarily to her mouth, and then to her heart, which has begun to pound. She looks intently at the wall.

The uneven lime wash throws up a face, barely visible, but mamma knows, she just knows in her bones that this is no trick of the light. Baby Blue gurgles and quickens his crawl. Mamma half slides and half crawls towards Blue. She grabs him just as he reaches the end of the floor, a finger just short of touching the wall.

In that split second, the face on the lime wash recedes to reveal a blurry image of a woman sitting bolt upright on a floor just like hers. Mamma clutches Blue and shuts her eyes, her body trembles, she feels fear oozing out from her skin as hot anger runs down her heart. Whoever or whatever it is had better not come near her baby.

When she opens her eyes again, everything is ordinary once more, even though her baby laughs his innocent baby laugh at someone on the wall and waves his baby Krishna doll at her, or it. She notices a change coming over Baby Blue Bottom. She sees him looking at his Krishna doll like he is having a silent conversation with it. Baby Blue sees it turning its head to wink at him and laugh but mamma sees nothing.

Baby Blue's eyes flip from his doll to the woman on the wall and back. His face suddenly grows serious. As if he has realised that this is not a game. Something about the woman, the way she is staring like she wants to plunge right into their room and consume them, makes him feel uncertain. For the first time Baby Blue experiences the feeling of wariness, the instinct of small prey. The afternoon turns chilly. He retreats into mamma's warm soft breasts. She enfolds him in her arms, and opens her blouse for him.

Later that night, when baba has eaten his dinner and they are sharing their quiet hour with Baby Blue on his baby mattress covered by a hand quilted sheet on their bed, when both have their hands on Blue's chest and tummy, mamma whispers her discontent with the house.

'There is something here. Something unnatural,' she says. 'There is a petni here, I am sure of it. We should find another house to live in.'

'Wha-at!' says baba, incredulous and amused at the same time. Whoever believes in petnis and other she-ghosts these days? 'Where did you get such a funny idea?'

'Not a funny idea,' mamma's voice rises a little. 'I know what I experienced today. I have been feeling watched for so long, even before he was born. I told you once or twice before.'

'Yes,' baba shrugs.

Women see and feel things that men do not, sometimes

even those that do not exist. He decides to give her his big news, instead of waiting for the weekend. 'Yes, we will have to shift house. I've just been told that I'll be kicked upstairs,' he says, naming a happening metropolis far from their sleepy B-class city.

The night has grown thick outside her window. The woman is getting ready for bed, when she hears the word petni. She starts. Her eyes involuntarily look at the dark sky outside. She feels the word hurtling towards her with ghoulish mirth.

'Petni' hits her ears like a vial of poison, infecting her from within. She rushes to the mirror to see her face. Tears well up and leak from her stricken eyes. She clamps her hand over her mouth to stop the wracking sobs that threaten to erupt.

'Petni.' That woman had called her a petni.

'Am I?' she asks herself. 'What have I become?'

For a long time afterwards, she shuts her mind to Baby Blue and his family.

Days slip past, followed by night. Baby Blue's world expands. He has begun to look up at the sky, especially the moon. There is a song that thakuma and mamma sing, though never together, when they hold him under the sky in the evening, and the moon is up.

Aae aae chand mama tip diye ja. Aamar chander kopale Chand tip diye ja

'Come, come O uncle moon. Come and put a dot. O moon put a dot on the forehead of my own moon.'

Today, it is baba who carries Blue in his arms out to where the evening is busy moistening the grass. They stand under a purple sky. Venus winks at them from above. Soon other stars start venturing out. Yellow Champa flowers glisten in the growing dark, their perfume heavy in the air. A solitary gecko chuckles to itself on the garden wall. The fireflies catch Blue's attention. His dark eyes dart from one flitting firefly to the next.

Mamma joins them in the garden. Then some friends of baba's passing by stop to chat. They come in to admire the garden. They remark how big Blue has grown. They chat about this and that. After a while, Baba goes somewhere with one of his friends. They soon return with two big bags. One bag clinks and feels cold when Blue tries to grab it, while the other steams and smells of food, and his nose twitches with interest.

Baba switches on the tape recorder. Music wafts out into the garden, surrounding them all. Blue moves his hands to the beat of the music. Everybody laughs. One of the women in the group cuddles him. Blue laughs too. They drink something from glass mugs, which Blue finds interesting. He leans forward to see and smell better, and hopefully get a taste, much to the amusement of the grown-ups. Mamma joins the drinking party. But she and the other women have only one mug each. Baba and the other men have many more.

Blue is given a brown liquid in his feeding bottle. The liquid looks frothy inside. It also looks interesting. Blue takes a sip. It is sweet and it tickles his tongue.

'Mmmm. Ga. Gmmm.' Says Blue.

'Hey, look at him drinking coke. He'll graduate to bigger stuff soon!' jokes an uncle.

'Like father like son,' jokes an aunty.

Everybody finds the jokes funny. Blue finds the conversation funny too. He likes the evening. There are so many people around him. Everybody is happy. But the happiest person in the garden is a Gublu-mamu. His jokes are the loudest. His songs are the most tuneful. And, he has tossed Blue into the air and caught him safely many times. Then afterwards, when they all go inside for dinner, it is Gublu-mamu who feeds Blue from his plate. It is Gublu-mamu who talks to him all the time. Gublu-mamu gives him water to drink. And, Gublu-mamu sings to him, lulls him to sleep. Blue makes up his mind to love Gublu-mamu the most, after mamma and baba.

Gublu-mamu returns again and again to meet Blue. When baba goes out of town for work related trips, it is he who drives mamma and Blue to the market, and helps them load the groceries into the car. Once when Blue had a fever, and baba was away, mamma telephoned him. Gublu-mamu came hurrying back from office in the middle of the day, and bundled them into baba's car. He took them to the paediatrician, looking more worried than mamma.

The misery on his face when Blue wailed as the doctor examined his tongue, made mamma laugh. The lady doctor smiled and told Gublu-mamu he would get used to these things once he became a father. But Gublu-mamu still looked doubtful. He stopped on their way back to buy Blue a lollipop. Mamma scolded him for spoiling Blue.

Blue is thinking of Gublu-mamu one bright morning when he notices a new photo on the wall opposite his bed. The photo is of a fat man with a beard and large eyes, sitting cross-legged on deerskin. Blue doesn't know what deerskin is. Nor does he recognise the trishul in his hand. To Blue, he looks like Gublu-mamu in a funny costume. He gurgles with pleasure. The man in the photo looks at him quizzically. He shakes his head in mock exasperation.

'Am I so easily replaced, little one?'

The voice is deep, yet a whisper riding a draft of morning breeze. Blue watches transfixed. Something within him answers, 'How is that possible?'

'It is not. And you are wise, my precious. The faces may change, but I remain. I cannot be replaced.'

From another part of the house Blue can hear a joyous hymn. It is the Mahamrityunjay Mantra being played on mamma's stereo player. The short hymn will be sung one hundred and eight times, and mamma will not turn it off until the very end. Mamma likes to listen to the Mahamrityunjay mantra in the mornings, and so does baba, even though he never enters mamma's puja room. The hymn, repeating over and over again with its accompanying music, fills the house with an uplifting vibe. It makes Baby Blue Bottom want to dance.

Now he reaches his chubby hands towards the photo on the wall. He gurgles and laughs. He is not alone in his joy. One by one happy little beings surround him. The room sparkles like a million broken sunbeams.

Blue feels the gush of happiness coursing through his little body. He sits upright on his mattress on the big bed. His mattress is covered with an oilcloth. A hand-quilted sheet covers the oilcloth. Something damp spreads beneath him. And he no longer feels comfortable. The fat man with the trishul smiles on benignly, a holy photograph on the wall.

Blue is no longer interested. He does not care about the photograph. His skin has begun to prickle. He does not like it, even as he acknowledges to himself that he should not have wet the bed.

Mamma has bought a little red, plastic potty for him. She has also been diligently making him sit on it every half an hour. Blue knows he is supposed to pee in it and poop in it. Mamma is very happy when he does. She never fails to make a big deal of him. The first time he peed in the plastic potty, mamma called up baba at his office to tell him. Then she called up all her friends to give them the news. Then she made a couple of long-distance calls to make sure his grandparents and aunts and uncles knew about it.

More often than not, Blue cannot be bothered. He would rather wear the potty on his head like a hat. This makes baba laugh, and he teases mamma. Mamma does not find it funny. But she always finds it hard to be annoyed with Blue for long. Blue knows this. Just as he knows that he should not wet his bed. So, he decides to give her twenty seconds before he lets her know that he hates wet beds.

'Waaaa...Waaa...Waaaa,' he wails.

'Oh Honey. My sugar baby. No. You baddy baby. Wet the bed again. But you're still mamma's honey baby...'

Blue listens to the gibberish. That's his mamma fussing over him. He likes being fussed over. Over time he has realized that he is supposed to be fussed over. But sometimes it gets on his nerves. Like the time he tried to climb down the stairs, and mamma insisted on cuddling him and cooing at him. He had said, 'Thap' to Mamma then, and kicked her as hard as he could.

He enjoys the way baba fusses over him though. There is a lot more adventure when baba fusses over him. Like carrying him on his broad shoulders and taking long strides at the same time. And, throwing him up in the air, only to catch him deftly again.

Mamma has made Blue dry and snug again. She puts him down on the pram and takes off the hand-quilted sheet, as well as the oilcloth to air his mattress. Then she wipes the oilcloth with a rag soaked in diluted Dettol water. She places it carefully on Blue's mattress. She covers it up with a fresh hand-quilted sheet. Then she smiles at Blue, who has been watching her with rapt attention.

'I'll wet it again. So that's a waste of work,' he says to himself.

Mamma thinks he looks adorable. She kisses his face. Then she wheels him out of the room. Once they reach the dining room, Mamma peels a banana and gives it to Blue. She watches him proudly as he chomps his way through the whole banana.

Mamma sings as she does her housework. There is a lot of

housework to be done. There's the food to be cooked. The bric-a-brac dusted. Plants watered and pruned. Tomcat shooed away. Maid supervised and yelled at. Clothes to be folded. Clothes to be bundled and sent to the Dhobi. Mamma seems to work throughout the day. And, she always sings while she works.

Blue likes to watch her as she goes about her daily chores. Sometimes he tries to participate. So, mamma always keeps some toys handy to distract him. Blue likes to watch mamma pick the grit out of the dal most of all. The dal is always colourful. The colour changes every day. One day it is yellow, the next day pink, then ochre, then brown, then white, and then yellow all over again. Mamma knows he likes watching her pick the dal clean. She chats with him while she does her work.

Blue is not interested in Mamma's conversation. He is watching the tomcat on the windowsill swishing his tail. He would like to catch that tail. But it is too high up for him. So that will have to wait till he can climb up on the chair.

'Hem,' says Blue.

Mamma thinks he is participating in her conversation. She calls him her honey baby. She reaches out to kiss him. Blue sticks out his foot for her to kiss. Mamma kisses his toes. Blue enjoys the sensation. He promptly gives her his other foot to kiss.

'My Gopali Gopiloo Gopala,' coos mamma.

'Ga doo da ba,' replies Blue.

Baba comes home for lunch. Blue gets excited. He throws his arms and legs about. He tries to step off the couch where he has been sitting for the past half an hour, waiting for Baba. He fails, tumbles, falls, and bawls.

'Oh baby, baby...' Mamma is almost in tears.

'He's ok,' says Baba, swinging Blue up in his arms. 'Right beta? He's a big boy now. That fall won't hurt him much. Besides, the couch is only a foot higher than the floor.'

Mamma is not convinced. She touches Blue's head feeling for bumps and bruises. She feels angry with baba when he accuses her of fussing too much. Baba says that boys will be boys. Mamma says that he is only a baby, and he has lots of time to become a boy later. Then baba says that he must learn while he is young. And, mamma says not so young. Then baba says, and mamma says, and baba says again and mamma says again... Blue decides it is high time he shut them up.

'Ba,' says Blue, looking directly at baba.

Both mamma and baba stop talking, and look at him.

'Did you hear that?' says baba proudly. 'He called me baba.'

'That's a fluke,' says mamma, jealous because Blue didn't say 'ma' instead. 'He only said 'ba.' Not baba!'

'Baabbaa,' says Blue again to Baba. 'Thoo,' he says to mamma.

'Thoo to you too,' says mamma, and flounces out of the room.

'My big beta. My strong beta.' Baba bounces Blue on the couch.

Blue agrees with baba. He is big and strong. Mamma should not molly-coddle him so much. Just the other day a gecko's dropping had landed close to him. He had wanted to pick it up to taste and find out what it was like. But no, mamma would not let him. Instead, she had shrieked and picked him up. Then she created a big hullabaloo about the maid's sloppy work. The maid was drinking her tea at that time.

Mamma's yelling made her bang the steel glass of tea on the hard cement floor. She picked up the offending dropping with her thumb and index finger. Lucky maid, Blue thought, ruefully. Then she tossed the un-tasted morsel at the tomcat, which promptly took flight, twitching tail, and all. The maid walked off without even washing her glass!

Blue heard about the maid's misdeeds throughout the week. So did baba. As well as the landlord's daughter, who sometimes came down to gossip ('and nose around the house,' according to mamma) and the whole retinue of their friends and their friends' friends! Blue had been aghast at mamma's ferocious reaction to a little black thing. Until, baba finally lost his temper with mamma. So 'thoo' to mamma.

Blue bites Baba's nose affectionately. Baba laughs and shakes his head. He tosses Blue up in the air. Then catches him again, like a ball.

'Next month you'll be a real big boy, son. We'll throw a big party to celebrate that. Won't we?'

Blue does not understand what 'party' means. But he agrees with Baba anyway. Besides, baba always comes up with good ideas. Whatever this party thing might be, it is bound to be good. Blue laughs to show his appreciation.

It is lunchtime soon. Baba feeds Blue his dal and rice. Blue never creates a fuss when baba feeds him. Blue feels special when baba feeds him. Mamma does it every day, so it is good to create a diversion with her. Baba feeds him every now and then, but each time he does he makes so many faces, and so many sounds with his mouth, and so many shapes out of the dal and rice, that Blue always finishes his food.

Lunch over. Blue watches mamma and baba eat. He dozes off in his high chair, before they are through. He does not realize when he has been transferred to his bed. He sleeps deeply in the afternoon. Without dreaming a single dream.

Later in the afternoon, Blue finds mamma and baba snuggling in bed. He and his bedding have been conveniently shifted to the side against the wall. He does not mind. His toes feel cool when he kicks at the wall. His eyes pick out patterns on the chalky surface of the wall. And, sometimes when he can manage it, especially when mamma's not looking, he gets to taste the chalky-lime taste of the wall.

4

Mamma and baba are busy discussing the details of his birthday. Blue has taken advantage of their lack of attention and enjoyed many licks of the wall. Now he sucks his thumb lazily, as he hears his name being mentioned for the umpteenth time. He feels good. This is the best afternoon of the week apart from Sunday. Blue does not know the names of the days yet. But he can recognize a Saturday when it comes. Mamma seems more relaxed, and baba whistles as he shaves.

Saturdays are half-holidays for baba. That means he is home for lunch, and a long cosy afternoon nap with Blue and mamma. After which they chat for a while at the dining table. Blue drinks his milk, and mamma and baba drink tea. Baba loafs around the house with Blue, while mamma gets ready. Then they go to the bazaar to buy groceries for the week. The air is cool, but the night is still very far away, when baba starts his car.

Blue and mamma occupy the front seat with baba. The shopping bags, egg case, Blue's water bottle, extra diapers and an extra set of clothes ('just in case there's an emergency,' is mamma's logic, to which baba's retort always is, 'why not pack a suitcase!') occupy the back seat.

Blue likes going to the bazaar. It is crowded and colourful. Big, dusty cows drop their dung as they stroll around and ruminate. Orange dogs sniffing around the stalls get chased by the stall owners, and they in turn chase the cats, but more out of a sense of duty than out of revenge. There are some goats as well, chewing leaves and dislodging pellets at the same time with a scholarly air. Pot-bellied vegetable sellers in bright lungis sit behind heaps of shiny green, red, purple, yellow, white, and brown vegetables.

Turbaned fruit sellers with curling moustaches swish their fly swatters disinterestedly. Boisterous tatterdemalions dig their noses. The banana men stand guard over their trolleys of yellow and green bananas, spitting out red betel juice every time they are told the bananas cost too much.

Blue likes them all. It makes him feel he is a part of one big family. Especially when the hawkers in the bazaar pay attention to him, and try to give him a tit-bit. Mamma always refuses those tit-bits. And to make matters worse, from Blue's point of view, baba completely agrees with her.

The gaudily dressed egg women never fail to attract Blue's attention. Mamma says they look disreputable, and never lets Baba buy the eggs. She bargains with them. Blue would like to play with their bead necklaces and ear-rings. They always smile and talk to Blue. But Mamma doesn't let their grimy hands go anywhere near him.

'Not fair,' grumbles Blue to himself as he piddles into his diaper for the third time.

Baba carries Blue around, while mamma haggles. Sometimes baba sets him down on the bare ground. Baba holds his hand while Blue swaggers and lurches at the same time, on the dusty and, very often, muddy bazaar grounds.

Mamma looks up from her haggling when Blue does this. Mamma loves to watch Blue walk. She also has a mortal fear of him falling on the 'germ-ridden,' filthy ground. Her face looks comical as she looks at Blue tenderly and tries to glare at Baba at the same time.

'Tha, tha, thap,' says Blue to get mamma's whole attention. Mamma melts into a kiss for him.

When mamma has purchased enough to fill all the shopping bags and some more to spare, baba takes them to a fast-food shop for kathi rolls and colas. Blue does not get any kathi rolls. Instead, he gets cola at room temperature. He also gets melted ice cream, but that is a summer time luxury. Blue prefers ice cream, even though he has eaten it only twice during his whole life. The first time was a few spoons full from Mamma's cup at a wedding almost four months ago. The second occasion was at Gublu-mamu's behest, about a month ago. But he remembers the taste so well, that he never fails to point at the freezer in the fast-food shop, every time they stop there for snacks. Mamma never fails to remark how intelligent Blue is to which baba gives his unfailing response, word for word the same as the first time; 'he has inherited your looks and my brains. Isn't that a blessing?'

Blue sucks his cola-at-room-temperature through a straw. He looks at the people looking at him with round eyes. These are the gawkers. There are always gawkers around Blue when he drinks his cola in a public place. Blue enjoys the attention. Sometimes he blows into the bottle, which he holds with both his hands, in order to show off. The cola bubbles up with a popping sound. This feat never fails to impress both Blue and his audience.

Blue prefers the men gawkers to the women gawkers. The women always come up to him and try to pinch his cheeks or talk gibberish with him. The men keep a respectful distance while they stare and smile, and sometimes whistle at him. This last response always makes Mamma mad.

'As if he's a dog,' she tattles to baba.

'There are some similarities, you know,' replies baba mischievously.

Mamma's eyes sparkle with a retort. Then she catches the meaning in Baba eyes, and ends up blushing instead. Blue burps. A woman gawker comes up to him and coos. She tries to touch his cheeks and hands. Blue decides it is time for some action.

'Ta Tai ta,' says Blue and takes a last sip from his cola. He stretches out his little arms towards her.

The woman gawker beams at mamma as she takes Blue in her arms. Blue dribbles his last mouthful of cola down her cleavage.

Mamma and baba laugh as they get into the car. They carry on giggling as baba drives out of the bazaar and turns into the ill-lit road that will take them home. The second-hand Premier Padmini car bumps along the badly tarred, pot-holed road. Blue stretches his legs and yawns.

'Oh no. No falling asleep now, you wee widdle bwat,' says mamma shaking him gently. 'Look, baby, look at those lights.'

Blue looks, not at the lights, but at Baba's hands on the

wheel. He wants to turn the wheel and slam his open palm on the horn. But like most things it is still too far away. His eyes are caught by the light of a passing car. The lights dance on the windscreen of their car. Then like the spark of a spitting firecracker, something falls on the windscreen. It is small and vile, and pulsating with desire. It does not wish to leave and is desperately looking for something to enter, something that can receive it, host it. The thing is a being, and it petrifies Blue even though he is in mamma's arms.

Blue is unable to shriek. He is unable to shut his eyes. He can do nothing but stare back at this being staring at him so hatefully. It is a tiny blob of hate. A slimy ball of fear. It is a creature of the spirit realm and it is being pulled away by a long shadowy arm, that to mamma and baba would appear to be nothing more harmful than wood smoke from an open fire nearby. Blue feels it wants to come in. Desperately wants to be let in. Inside Blue. It locks on to Blue. It tries to will him to leave. Tries to jolt him out. Out into the vast nothingness. Alone with the shadow lurking, ready to pounce. So that it can come inside him and live in his body.

Blue stiffens in mamma's lap. Her arm instinctively holds him closer to her bosom, and the palm of her hand pats his small chest rhythmically. A part of Blue feels protected, but a cry dislodges deep within Blue nevertheless, and rises in silent supplication. The voice responds immediately, falling on him like a caress.

There is nothing to fear here my little one. What you have just witnessed is nothing but what in your world is called death. This was a sudden death. The man who died was unwilling, even though his time had come. Death is nothing but a transition. There is nothing to fear.

A light, like a wand, sweeps the shadow away. Sweeps the lost being away. Bathes Blue in a halo of love again. Blue looks at the receding arc of light. A weight seems to lift off him. He leans back on mamma's soft lap. The world around him returns to the earthly shapes and colours that Blue is increasingly getting used to. Just as he is seeing less and less of the other world, and his memory of his life from there is fading.

'Those strobe lights are coming from a police car,' says baba grimly. 'Something must have happened down this road. We'd better get home quickly.'

Mamma looks out of the window a little fearfully. Baba presses his foot harder on the accelerator.

The morning's newspaper dispels the mystery. The members of a rival gang killed a well-known hoodlum the night before. Baba calls mamma from the kitchen to show her the news. Mamma is very excited. She cannot wait to tell all her friends that they went past the exact spot, exactly when this horrible deed was being committed. Well almost, but that is good enough to keep everyone talking, and telling them what a narrow escape they have had. As for Blue, it is as if nothing ever happened. Beams of sunlight flood the dining room, showering hundreds of happy, frolicking miniscule Gopalas all around Blue. But they make tomcat sneeze. And, they make Mamma complain about the maid who has done a sloppy job sweeping the house. Otherwise, how can there be so much dust floating around every time the sun comes into the room!

5

Today is the *day*. Today is Blue's first birthday. He does not quite realize this. Though he can feel the excitement and tension. Mamma's been after everybody for three days now. Blue's made many happy trips to as many shops with mamma and baba. Buying clothes, ordering the cake, shopping for balloons, streamers, paper plates and cups... Blue crawls across the bed. Mellow sunlight tints his curls with gold.

'Hey there. Easy now. I know you are a big boy today,' says baba as he picks Blue up.

Blue's eyes sparkle with excitement. No, today is just not like a normal, everyday, day. Today is special. Baba is not supposed to be reading the paper in bed till so late. Today something big is going to happen. And, he is a part of that something big. A big part.

'Tea, tea!' Yells Baba.

'Thee. Thee. Thee!' yells Blue in glee.

'Yes sir. Yes sir,' sings mamma from deep inside the kitchen.

Mamma comes in, holding a steaming cup of tea for Baba and a glass of lukewarm milk for Blue. She hands the tea to baba and places the milk on a plywood tea chest painted white and turned upside down to serve as a bedside table. She takes Baby Blue in her arms. She kisses and cuddles him. She rubs her nose on his belly button. Blue shrieks with laughter.

'Today is mamma's honey baby's birthday. Mamma's baby is a big boy,' croons mamma.

Then off goes Blue with mamma to the kitchen, which smells nice. Many good things are cooking in it. Tomcat is sitting on the sill, washing his paws in anticipation.

'Meow...Meow, meow.' Pleads tomcat.

'Ow. Ow. Ow,' says Blue.

'Alright. Alright,' says Mamma. 'Here's a chicken bone for you. There's still a lot of meat left in it. Don't think I'm giving you leftovers.'

Tomcat bolts with the chicken bone. But he is back again after a few minutes. Tomcat watches Blue as he finishes his milk. Blue holds the glass with both hands, and tilts his head back as he tries to drink to the last drop. Mamma, who is supporting the glass lightly with her left-hand, laughs. Blue watches tomcat over the rim of his glass. He feels bigger. A few more days and he'll be able to catch tomcat's tail. Tomcat seems to catch Blue's thought. He swishes his tail menacingly, and murmurs a soft warning. Mamma shoos tomcat away. Then she throws another chicken bone after him as a mark of forgiveness.

Blue spends the rest of the day amidst a lot of excitement and fuss. In between his bath, lunch, and a short nap, he watches many people come and go. Gublu-mamu is the only one who stays put. Blue watches him blow the balloons up one by one. Gublu-mamu gives him a balloon. Blue clutches it, feeling very important. The landlord's daughter helps Baba put up the streamers. The maid, cheerful and ever ready to work for once, rearranges the drawing room furniture. She brings in the chairs from the dining room and lines them up against the wall. The couch and the armchairs occupy the opposite wall. Some loose chairs borrowed from the landlord fill up the gaps in between. The maid looks at Blue, claps her hand and gives him a toothy smile. Blue stares back at her, he has never seen such red teeth and black gums before. His lower lip trembles with fear. Gublu-mamu sends the maid off on some errand before her cheerfulness can do further damage.

Blue falls asleep in the middle of the streamers and balloons, on the floor. He dreams, not of his erstwhile playmates and the voice that always wraps him in so much love, but of Gublu-mamu, and the balloons, the wrappers, mamma's arms, and baba's lap, bouncing him and bouncing him, until it's just like the brand-new baby rocking chair on which he was made to sit and rock, with baba and Gublu-mamu taking turns to make sure he stays put, only better! Someone carries him off to bed, and when he wakes, there are three pairs of loving eyes looking at him.

Blue is all dressed up for the party. It is not really a

children's party, despite the balloons, streamers, and cake. There are only three more children, all more or less Blue's age. The rest of the people in the room are grown-ups. They are busy talking and laughing among themselves. Baba and most of the uncles in the room are drinking that interesting smelling stuff that Baba calls beer. Mamma and the aunties are drinking orange squash. Children's nursery rhymes and birthday party songs are playing on the tape recorder. But nobody's listening to the songs. Not even Blue and his friends.

Suddenly baba makes an announcement, seconded by Gublu-mamu. Mamma gets busy, trying to rewind the cassette to the exact spot where the song 'It's A Hap-Hap-Happy Birthday' is located. Everybody leaves his or her seat to converge at the dining table. Blue rides on Gublu-mamu's shoulder to the dining table. He is made to sit on his high chair. The cake glistens directly in front of him. The candle, which is a wax replica of the numeric one, waves its flame like a flag.

Mamma puts her arm around Blue possessively. Baba stands next to him. Everybody is exhorted to sing 'Happy Birthday.' They all oblige. Mamma and baba clasp Blue's right hand. The three of them blow out the candle together. They bring Blue's hand down on the cake. Much to Blue's surprise, the knife in his hand goes through the cake. He promptly makes a mental note of this fascinating new tool for future use.

Gublu-mamu makes sure Blue gets more than his fair share of the cake. He constantly takes pictures of him being fed the cake. First by Mamma, then by Baba, then by the landlord's daughter, and sundry other aunties who make Blue their excuse for getting their pictures taken. Blue passes from lap to lap. He gets a paper package from each lap he visits, but Mamma promptly puts them away.

Everybody has something to say to him. Blue is the star of the show. He is one whole year old, even though he neither knows nor cares. What matters is he is the centre of their universe.

The party gets more and more boisterous after the cake cutting ceremony. Blue gets lost in the melee of people. He finds a balloon and holds on to it for dear life. Another baby toddles up to him and tries to snatch the balloon away. Blue screams. The other baby screams. They dig their fingers into the balloon to get a better grip. The balloon bursts with a big bang. There is a moment's stunned silence in the room. Then the baby runs off bawling to her mother. Blue stands his ground, round-eyed. Everybody laughs, except for the bawler's mother. Baba gives the other baby a balloon. He gives Blue a balloon and a kiss.

The rest of the evening passes in a haze. People seem to be eating and drinking and talking and laughing at the same time. Blue finds this very fascinating. He does not want to go into the bedroom to change his diaper, because he does not want to miss anything. He goes to Baba, who has a glass of beer in his hand. Baba seats him on his knee. Blue leans back on Baba's chest, and listens to the conversation. The voices grow faint, and then fainter. The people in the room look more and more blurred. From a distance he hears Baba asking Mamma whether his bed is made or not. Then, blissful silence reigns.

The woman uncurls herself. Her jaw is set and almost crushing her teeth. Irritation tingles through her body. Her hair, a Medusa-head of salt and pepper waves, spreads around her face. Her skin has grown thick and there are bangles around her neck. Spontaneous joy is little more than the clink of small change. This is who she is now, but her mind living in the present, does not remember the transition.

When does a woman, a nice ordinary woman with hopes and dreams, turn into a ghoul? A petni. A creature created from the ashes of unfulfilled desires. Is it the lot of every woman to succumb to some form or the other of the 'petni?' Is she now one, at least in the metaphorical sense?

The woman shakes her head. She had forgotten how she had wept when she first heard the other woman calling her a 'petni.' A spark of anger ignites the afternoon. Who did she think she was?

'Stupid woman,' she mutters to herself. 'That stupid woman and her stupid piety and her stupid goody-goody life! She will learn. She will learn!'

She fumes and frets, until it becomes too exhausting. She chides herself for indulging her imagination too much. It is high time she stopped these unproductive mental wanderings. There is a real world outside. She has things to do there. And real people to meet. Baby Blue's dimpled smile floats up in her mind, and she pauses. Her own son is no longer a baby. He does not need her the way this baby needs his mother. That phase is over, she reminds herself. Her eyes turn steely. It is high time she lived for herself. Having let off steam, she lies flat on her back and stretches her arms and legs on either side, like she is making snow angels. The childish movement relaxes her. She is almost asleep when a half-remembered incident scampers like a mouse through her head. She stares at the ceiling.
It is not an incident, but the image of her own face and the

sound of her own laughter. Her eyes are bitter as she gazes at the room, the slow fan, the humming air conditioner, the chic looking bedroom furniture whose reflection bounces off the smooth granite tiles of the floor. She still thinks of the red oxide floor though, like one would an old ally who is no longer beside her. She lets the tears fall, because there is no one there to notice and embarrass her. The futility of it makes her weep more. How many afternoons has she spent like this? How many more will she spend like this?

Time can create such a sly amnesia that what seems like a minute can, in reality, be a decade.

The woman feels invisible these days, even to herself. The house she had kept clean and tidy was invisible to those she had nurtured it for. They lived in it and went away. The food she had cooked or planned and supervised in the kitchen was invisible. They had eaten their fill and gone, without noticing what they had consumed. Nobody has seen what she had done. And now she had ceased to see herself.

She had for a while lived the pipe dream of motherhood. But what were children really? Children were strangers one loved like a fool, believing one knew them and would learn more and more about them as they grew into adulthood, when all they did was grow and grow away, until they finally left for good. What are memories after all, but the coins in a beggar's collection tin?

She studies the solitaire on her thickened finger as she mulls and mulls. She rubs her back against the pile of the silk Kashmiri rug at the foot of her bed. It is a narrow piece in colours that match the counterpane and curtains. But it does not provide the comforting coolness of the bare red oxide floor. She slides off the rug and rolls away until she can touch the wall. She looks back at the story she had begun all those years ago, when she herself used to live in a small sleepy town-city in a rented house with furniture that she would not do up the servant's quarters with today. Where did all those afternoons go? Where are the people and places her mind had been with in its wanderings?

The woman hears someone's cell phone ringing. The sound is loud and has cut through the walls of her home. The ringtone is a musical chanting of the Mahamrityunjay Mantra, and it floats over her like petals borne on a breeze before sinking into the afternoon.

6

Blue, now almost two, sits in the middle of a vast muddle of toys. He stretches his legs. He holds the leg of a chair for support and stands up. He surveys his domain. The toys strewn around him are his subjects. He is the monarch. He cannot make up his mind about the toys; there are so many favourites to choose from. Mamma, who never seems to get tired of watching him run here and there, picks up a squeaky frog for him. Baba, who likes to watch him without appearing to, gives him a rubber telephone. Blue squeezes the frog. Then he chews the mouthpiece of the rubber phone. And then he throws them both to the floor and gurgles with laughter.

After a while the house begins to smell of incense. Blue recognizes this smell now. He tumbles forward as fast as he can to the prayer room. Mamma has her palms folded. Her eyes are closed. Blue drops to a crawl and creeps in from behind. Baba creeps right behind Blue. Blue raises his head, and finds himself staring straight at the other Baby Blue.

This Blue is blue all over. He has a peacock feather tied to his curly hair. He has lots of shiny things over his arms. Some of the ornaments are like the ones Mamma wears when she dresses up in shiny saris, and puts up her hair, and baba has to carry Blue because she finds it difficult to manage Blue when she is dressed like that. The other Blue has a bit of butter dribbling from his mouth. A slight smile curls around his bright pink lips, and the soles of his feet are red. This Blue always winks at Blue Bottom whenever their eyes meet. Blue is familiar with this Blue, because he has seen mamma praying and lighting lamps to the little images in her puja room below the calendar almost every day.

He also has his baby Krishna toy, a little worse for the wear, but still recognisable, and this Blue looks exactly like his toy. He has no memory of the time when he was too small to wriggle off, and mamma would place him on a thick soft mat next to her while she prayed. Nevertheless, Baby Blue is no stranger to mamma's evening ritual and the Blue God she loves so much. Mamma and Blue go through the ritual every day, but Blue's fascination never pales. Not least because he is not allowed to touch anything in the puja room.

Now the other Blue winks, like he always does. Blue Bottom winks back. The other Blue beckons slyly. Blue Bottom beckons back. He sticks his tongue out. Blue Bottom does the same. Then he stops with his tongue hanging out. He sees the universe unfurling on the other Blue's tongue. Blue Bottom stares hard. This whole business of stars and planets and whatnot on the other Blue's tongue has an oddly familiar ring to it. But he cannot put his finger to it. The memory hovers at the edge of his mind, only to slip away before he can remember. Like the woman on the other side, he too is caught in a cycle of *jamais vu* moments. His moments are tossed at him every time mamma prays. Piqued and a bit annoyed, Baby Blue inches forward to investigate.

Baba catches him by his belly, and hoists him up. Mamma laughs, stopping in the midst of her evening ritual.

'My widdle Gopala wants to play with that naughty butter thief Gopala? Mamma will get you a special Gopala. But you are my Gopala. My own real, live Gopala.'

'Gopala, Gopala,' thinks Blue. 'Mamma calls you that. But you also have other names...'

But Blue cannot remember them. And Gopala does not help him. He has gone back to being just a calendar on the wall — the inexpensive kind made of stiff glossy paper and garish colours. He is not even a proper calendar anymore. The pages containing the dates have long been torn off. Now he is the official cover-over-the-crack-in-the-wall. Mamma has a small brass image, in the same posture as the calendar Gopala, and this is the one she prays to. She also has some grown up versions of Gopala, each version has a different name. They all look serious. But one, in particular, appears to be very scary.

The prayer room looks ordinary again. A minute ago, Blue

thought that he had found his long-lost friend. He looks at the other again, for assurance. There is none. Then, Blue Bottom's attention is diverted again. Her evening prayers over, mamma is instructing baba about something. Blue listens to her excited chatter, and baba's good-humoured replies. Something is going to happen. Carried by mamma, he watches baba get a stout wooden stool from the shed in the garden, where the gardener keeps his tools and extra flowerpots, alongside an old rusty bicycle and a tin trunk or two. Baba sets it up under the loft and brings down a suitcase. Mamma joggles Blue in her arms, as she watches baba.

'No, not that one. That's too big. We should take two small ones,' she says when he pulls a large suitcase down.

Baba puts it back, and brings down another and then another. He dusts them with a rag. Mamma backs away, shielding Blue's mouth and nose gently with her hand. Blue, all agog, watches the proceedings. He points at the boxes.

'Gadum, gadum!' says Blue.

'Yes,' says baba. 'We are going gadum, gadum!'

'Not now. Day after tomorrow,' says mamma. 'We'll go gadum gadum!' She sets him down on the sofa and claps her hands. Blue claps in response.

Blue has no idea about today and tomorrow or the day after. He soon loses interest in the preparations, which is just as well for mamma and baba. However, the day after tomorrow does arrive at last, and mamma gets busy with the suitcases and the bags. Blue watches her suspiciously. He is also excited.

Baba has gone to office, but today mamma has not spent much time in the kitchen. Something is afoot. Baby Blue watches Mamma as she starts packing their clothes and other travel paraphernalia. His clothes, some soft toys and quilted sheets and rubber cloth go into one suitcase. Mamma and Baba's clothes fit into another. Mamma packs Baba's shoes and hers in individual polythene bags, which she then stuffs into a large nylon bag. Blue puts his sandals into the bag.

'You'll need those in the train, shona,' says Mamma, and takes them out again.

Blue brings his orange teddy bear. Mamma looks at him, shakes her head and stuffs the bear in along with the shoes. Blue brings his red train. Mamma laughs.

'You can't take all your toys with you, shona baba. We're are only going there for two weeks.'

'No!' says Blue, and stubbornly clutches his train. 'Twain.'

'No,' says Mamma firmly.

Blue's lower lip starts to tremble. He sniffs. His eyes fill up with tears. Mamma looks helplessly at him. She takes the train and puts it on the bed.

'No, baby,' says Mamma to Blue, in a surprisingly firm voice.

Baba walks into the room. He has just returned from work. He is on leave from today, but he had been to his office to finish some last-minute work. Blue runs up to Baba.

'Baba. Baba. Mamma,' complains Blue.

Baba laughs. He turns to Mamma. 'What have you done now?'

'I've done? Your son wants to pack all his toys! One would think we are emigrating, instead of going for a two-week holiday! I've packed his teddy bear and ball. And that's it. No more.'

'Baba, Baba,' says Blue wagging a fat finger at Mamma.

Baba puts Blue on the ground. 'You give this fellow his lunch. I'll do the packing. I know exactly what we need and what we don't.'

'Don't touch my clothes,' warns Mamma.

'Ha. Ha.' Laughs Baba. 'Why blame him?'

'Ha. Ha,' laughs Blue. 'Wa bame eem!'

Mamma hoists Blue on her hip, and flounces out of the room. Baba shakes his head at her retreating figure. Then he bends down to repack everything. Blue is not too interested in eating. Mamma's too distracted to force him. She is wondering what Baba's doing. Blue takes advantage of her lack of attention and drops some dal and rice on the floor.

'Bad boy. Very bad boy! Mamma won't love you!' Mamma wags her finger angrily at Blue.

Blue looks at her round-eyed. Mamma seems very testy today.

'Mamma, sowy,' lisps Blue. He tries to give her a kiss.

A bit of dal and a couple of grains of rice form a pattern on Mamma's cheek. Mamma takes Blue in her arms and feeds him by hand. Blue strokes her cheeks.

'All done,' says Baba cheerily, while he washes his hands at the basin in the corner of the dining room. 'Light and easy, that's the way to travel. You know less is more. Like when you wear nothing but your...'

'Shshsh!' remonstrates Mamma. 'Careful how you speak in front of him!'

'Mamma wa nuttin, mamma wa nuttin,' sings Blue.

Baba laughs. Mamma covers her face with her free hand. Her ears turn red.

They eat a simple lunch of dal, rice, and fried fish. Mamma does not want to do too much of washing up, so she has kept the food simple. She has fed Blue from her plate, instead of his own, and now proceeds to eat his left overs along with her lunch. The maid has been taking French leave since yesterday. Baba thinks she ought to be sacked but mamma is not so sure the next one will be any better. Baba adds some mango pickle to his plate. Mamma purses her lips but says nothing. She made the dal less spicy so all three of them can eat the same food, instead of making it separately for Blue.

Baba offers to wash up, while mamma packs Blue's biscuits, bananas, boiling hot water in a large flask, cooled boiled water in another similar flask, tin of milk powder, cereal, some chocolates, two bowls, two tumblers, cutlery and paper towels in a hamper. This is Blue's special hamper. It is a wide-bottomed woven plastic basket with a lid and handles. It is only used for carrying Blue's food, utensils and other small things necessary to keep a baby well and hygienically fed. Mamma is very particular about keeping it spotlessly clean. She never sets it down on the ground, especially outside the house. It is always placed on top of the other pieces of luggage when either she or Baba are not carrying it.

Blue finds his toy engine under a chair. He holds it aloft like a trophy.

'Choo, chooo,' says Blue to mamma, and he gives it to her to pack.

'Oh no. Now he wants his engine,' says mamma.

'Just stuff it into that big bag of yours, one small toy won't make much of a difference,' says Baba with his face averted.

Mamma looks at him suspiciously.

Blue looks at both with suspicion. He is sure Baba has done something to make mamma angry. Blue watches her face. He looks at baba again. Something is going on here. They are not talking, but Blue can feel the tension. Mamma unzips one of the bags. She frowns, and zips it up again. She rummages in the cupboard and stuffs some articles of clothing in the bag. Baba busies himself by putting Blue's shoes on for him. Blue is immediately distracted. He forgets about the crackle in the air between mamma and baba. These are Blue's favourite shoes. These are more like sandals, with Velcro fasteners. Blue wriggles his toes inside them. The Velcro makes a crackling noise. Blue likes the noise. He wriggles his toes again.

The clock's face shows that it is just one o'clock. The train does not come in before two thirty p.m., but that does not stop Gublu-mamu from puffing into the house, looking all hot and excited.

'Come on. Come on. The auto-rickshaws are waiting. Don't want them to charge extra for waiting, do you?' Gublu-mamu picks up the larger suitcase.

'It's too early,' protests mamma.

'What'll we do in the house now that we're all dressed and ready?' says Baba.

Gublu-mamu has already begun to load the suitcases and bags into one of the auto-rickshaws. 'I'll go in this one with the luggage. You guys follow in the other.'

This arrangement suits everybody, except Blue. He would rather go with Gublu-mamu, and reaches for him.

'Not now, hero,' laughs Gublu-mamu. 'I'll take you once we reach the station.' He turns to Baba. 'Did you remember to disconnect the car battery?'

Baba nods as he tries to refasten Blue's shoes. Blue has already kicked them off in a show of defiance. Baba takes a while to put them back on Blue's feet because he is struggling so much. Gublu-mamu takes this opportunity to whiz off in his auto-rickshaw. Blue lets out a wail of rage. Mamma and Baba can do nothing to stop him. The auto-rickshaw driver, waiting patiently for them, manages to divert Blue's attention by pulling funny faces at him, and they finally set off after Gublu-mamu's auto-rickshaw. Blue is in a good mood again, and everybody is relieved.

The auto-rickshaw shakes and rattles as it tries to catch up. Stray dogs run away squealing whenever it comes near touching distance of their tails. The afternoon sun beats relentlessly down. Gusts of hot, dry wind bring no respite from the heat. The melting tar on the road makes a squelching noise whenever the auto-rickshaw wheels run over the tar puddles. Mamma sneezes. Baba keeps mopping his face. The driver wipes a stray rivulet of sweat with his shirtsleeve. Blue leans back on Mamma's lap to enjoy the moving scenery better.

A picture of Lord Shiva, complete with trident and snake coiled around his matted hair is pasted on the windscreen of the auto rickshaw. A couple of wilted hibiscus flowers and a joss stick holder with burnt out joss sticks in it are balanced precariously in front of the picture of Shiva. Blue watches the fragrant ash disperse into the air every time the auto rickshaw lurches forward. He is intrigued by the benign smile on Shiva's face. He starts to smile back at Shiva, but he stops in mid smile. Shiva's smile arcs towards Blue. Like a rainbow. But Blue can barely see its colours, they are so pale in the afternoon light. He frowns at it. He tries to grasp its meaning. The rainbow brightens for a split second, as if to nudge a memory in Blue's mind. Then it flows back into the furrow of Shiva's brow. Blue gazes at the spectacle with round intense eyes. He gazes at the third eye on Shiva's forehead. The eye glows, and comes alive momentarily before becoming a painted eye on a printed picture again. Blue is bored with it already. The picture keeps throwing riddles at him, but it cannot hold his attention anymore. Its meaning and message are lost. It is not even an interesting puzzle anymore. He prefers to watch the scenery passing swiftly by, outside the auto.

There is not much by way of scenery. This used to be a town before getting ambitious and desiring the status of a city. The municipality has not been able to keep up with the progress. Open drains border the main roads on both sides. Flowering trees planted between long intervals spread their dusty, gnarled arms towards a hard-blue sky. A few shrivelled flowers stand testimony to the feeble efforts of the trees at beautification. Discoloured houses cluster at the edges. There are many high-rise buildings too. They look gaunt beside the red tiled bungalows surrounded by lush gardens that softly proclaim that there is wealth and beauty, beside the squalor in this growing town-city.

They reach the station in one piece, despite the auto-rickshaw driver's reckless driving. The train is an hour late, but this does not bother anybody — they would have been concerned had the train been on time. Many people arrive at the station late anyway, because the trains are late anyway. The grey cement floor of the station is mottled with betel-leaf juice, phlegm, chewing gum, and what looks suspiciously like urine, among other things. Groups of beggars and free trippers are sleeping on the station grounds. Nobody minds them. People just hop over them when they want to get across.

Mamma does not want Blue to walk there. She insists on carrying him. She also keeps an eagle eye open for Blue's hamper, lest some dirty urchin lays his germ-ridden hands on it.

Baba is busy with the man at the ticket counter. There seems to be some confusion regarding their tickets. The aunty with the balloon-snatching baby, along with her husband, enters the station with a great hustle and bustle. Mamma's face breaks into a smile when she sees them. Blue stares at the other baby with round eyes. The two ladies start talking almost immediately — about the dirty station, the holiday that they will be spending together, the clothes they plan to buy for the coming Durga festival, and so on and so forth.

The balloon-snatcher goes off with her father, who is going to where Baba is arguing with the ticket man about seating them all in one place. Baba is explaining to the man that they are all travelling together and Gublu-mamu is not a single traveller. The balloon-snatcher's father adds to baba's arguments. The man at the booth advises them to adjust with their fellow passengers, but baba wants the seat changed. The argument seems to be going nowhere. Mamma, holding Blue clumsily is keenly trying to catch all that is being said. The balloon-snatcher's mother is also distracted. Blue struggles in Mamma's arms. He has seen Gublu-mamu marching towards him, holding a red plastic dog on a plastic string.

'If you pull its tail, it will wobble and jump,' says Gublu-mamu. Blue watches entranced.

Gublu-mamu makes the dog wobble and jump. Blue lunges for Gublu-mamu's arms, and mamma lets go of him. Gublu-mamu catches him deftly with one arm. Mamma is secretly relieved that Gublu-mamu is here to look after Blue. She does not try to hold him back. Gublu-mamu makes the dog wobble and jump again. Blue wants to have a go. Gublu-mamu shows him how to, and Blue tries, but the dog doesn't move. Blue tries again and again with the same results. But he chortles with laughter all the same.

The train arrives, sending tremors all the way down to the end of the platform. Blue and his entourage, including the balloon-snatcher's family, wait patiently. They have reserved tickets in the A/C two-tier bogey. They can wait for the crowd to thin before getting in.

Gublu-mamu and baba and the balloon-snatcher's father load up the luggage and help Blue and mamma and balloon-snatcher and her mother get in. Gublu-mamu holds the door to the compartment open, squeezing his large body in the narrow space that leads to the two toilets. It is cool inside. Grey blue and cool. Many people come in and go out. Goodbyes are exchanged. Blue watches with round eyes. Some strangers look at him and smile. They also smile at the balloon-snatcher, but she is looking at Blue distrustfully. At last, the train heaves itself out of the station.

'Hooray! We are off!' says Gublu-mamu. He turns to the two babies and starts singing a popular Cliff Richard song, 'We are going for a summer holiday ay. We are going for a week or two...'

Baba and balloon-snatcher's baba also join in. And then mamma. Her voice is sweet and mellow. To Blue it is the closest sound to the voice from the deep he has not been hearing lately. Gublu-mamu starts to dance in the narrow space between the two seats. Blue rocks on baba's lap. He wants to dance too. The train picks up speed on the long sunlit railway track. Their stop on that sunlit track is a resort town with golden beaches, turquoise seas, and plates of seafood, gallons of beer, a bunch of dear friends and sandcastles to be built for a baby or two. In short, a straight track to happy times.

7

The sunlit rail track is little better than the road leading back to Blue's house from the bazaar. Indeed, it is more treacherous, because it looks so straight and shiny, racing over a bed of stones that wink back at the sun despite their speckled grey colour. But things can go astray. Like missing fishplates. Or a crack in the iron rail. Anything can happen.

Afterwards time becomes static, a circular chasm.

There must necessarily always be a cause before the effect, like missing parts or cracked things. But the medley of people in a train are nothing other than casualties. They just happened to be there. Their deaths of course will have an effect, at least for a while. The loss of human lives will grab headlines in the newspapers and take prime time slot on TV. For a while. There will be retribution after that, perhaps. For the lives lost and the lives ruined.

Afterwards, like pond water converging over a stone thrown by a sulky, truant schoolboy, this tragedy, too, will be submerged by the waters of time.

Through the mangle of flesh and bone and twisted metal, Blue hears the voice:

This life is a deathlike existence to those who were hitherto free-floating souls. Ultimately, all are part of the seeming chaos of the cosmos, and all long to return. But forget as they live, that this life is just a phase in their existence.

Blue feels bereft. He is not the only one listening. There are so many. But it is all in a state of disquiet. Blue leans voice-wards, like a sailor on a shipwreck, leaning towards the rescue boat in a stormy sea, hailing him.

Time has turned into a void. It has no rhythm now. No routine. No motion. Time is now a gentle undulation in the Great Cosmic Lake.

Blue Bottom can see the path, but he is too shell-shocked to realize where he is supposed to be headed. He feels he is being squeezed and pushed down a tunnel. Everything is dark around him. He cannot stop his movement. A great force is pushing him out and he is not strong enough to fight it. He is terrified. The mass of petrified people, the blood and gore, the viciously flickering flames. All he can do is watch helplessly. He is not a part of it. It is no longer a touchable, feel-able thing. Between him and them, lies a thick jelly-like silence. A foggy chasm he cannot cross.

The room is dark and shadowy. Mamma's face is covered with bandages. She is moaning. Baba is weeping silently, his head bowed. The other people in the room are silent and shadowy. The only sound is grief's soft footfall.

Blue Bottom finds Gublu-mamu looking at mamma and baba. His face radiates love and sorrow and peace all at the same time. He looks at Blue, his face glowing with infinite understanding. Blue feels very close to Gublu-mamu. He feels they share a bond that even mamma and baba cannot breach. He makes a move towards Gublu-mamu. He tries to reach him. But Gublu-mamu smiles his smile of infinite understanding and with an energy burst of love, stops Blue Bottom from reaching out. Then he's gone in a blur of light.

Blue is alone in a room full of grieving people. Their grief flows in a trickle towards him. The trickle soon becomes a tide. He finds himself thrashing in the tide. He finds himself engulfed. He will either be suffocated by it or he will dissolve in it. Unless he can get away. Break free. Shake it off.

Blue struggles like a drowning being, fighting the pull of that turbulent ocean, fighting to be free. Something wrenches. The pain terrifies him. There is utter darkness. Blue feels like a buoy floating aimlessly in a void in an endless journey to nowhere. The uncertainty torments Blue, and there is no voice to ease his anguish. Finally, he feels a tug and is pulled steadily, and gently towards a place he can neither see nor comprehend. He can only sense that it is there, that it exists. Peace and wellbeing flow into him like pure dawn air. He begins to hear the voice again, first as a whisper and then, steadily louder, clearer.

Baby Blue Bottom is the duck returning to shore. He has managed to shake off the water from his back. It is time for him to fly. It is time for him to remember. The voice calls him, and as he listens, his memory returns. Mamma and baba's searing grief begins to wilt and peel away, falling off him like withered leaves or dead feathers. The Voice becomes a translucent shape of glowing light, surrounding Blue, rocking him. Ever so gently. The Lotus rock of mamma's arms. Then it seeps into him. Flows into him like milk. Like the nourishing milk from mamma's nipples, and he knows he has come back home...

The afternoon is all around her, in splinters. The sharp pieces of the destroyed day pierce her skin like poison darts. The woman writhes on the floor.

'No! No! No!' she screams, without sound. Her denials erupt inside her head and spread their hot lava.

Her eyes are bursting with tears that refuse to flow. Her eyes want to punish her. She gets up with a violent shift of her body. Her hair loose and wild, eyes darting, as if looking for a way to escape from a hundred adversaries. Her shoulders convulse as she buries her face in her hands.

'What am I thinking? How can I think this way?' The words slip out, audible now, though a whisper, as if someone else is speaking to her, from inside her own body.

Only a bad mother imagines her baby dead. She slaps her forehead with her open palm. Once. Twice. Thrice. She is a bad mother. Bad. Bad. Bad!

Thinking such thoughts is as good as invoking the devil. Or becoming a petni! That woman was right to call her one. She deserves it. How could she? How could she? But once, she very nearly had.

She remembers with a juddering shudder how she had once thrown her five-month-old baby down. All those years ago. It was another afternoon, and she had been alone. Alone for too long. Away from her office and at home. For too long. Too long. The memory grips her like a python's stranglehold. Holding her throat, she gasps but the memory will not let go.

She recalls feeling insane after a bout of lullabies that she had sung to her sleepless baby with increasing exasperation. The walls of the house seemed to bend down towards her with wicked intent. Her anger had neither form nor colour nor scent. It had sprouted in her heart with the suddenness of a wild mushroom in the rain. She had not even understood it fully.

Her action had taken place in a split second. But

within that split second, the split of the split second had turned her arm a fraction of an inch in the right direction. Her baby's little body had hit the spring mattress of the bed and not the hard cement floor.

The baby, her baby, so small and helpless, totally dependent on her, had sensed her rage and cried. It had taken her another few seconds to grasp what she had done, and she had flung herself on the bed, over her baby, whimpering, crying, 'Oh, my God! What have I done... was going to do?! How? Oh, my God! Oh, baby! Oh, my baby!'

Her baby was unhurt, and she was overcome with relief. She remembers holding her baby close. Giving him her breast. Her baby, never doubting his mother's love, had latched on to her breast, and fallen asleep soon after.

The woman had slipped into quietude as her baby slept, comforted by her nursing. How comforting it was to her as well, to feel his tender pull on her nipple, as if he was draining the pain and anger out of her, his gentle heartbeat against her ribcage, his baby smell wafting around her. It had occurred to her then and there, that the seemingly mindless, physical things she had to do daily when she took care of her baby, was like a meditative ritual. It was like prayer in deeds. It was the closest she had ever come to the gates of the divine.

How could she have even thought of flinging her own baby away, then? And how has she ended up imagining another baby's death, a violent death, now? She shudders again.

'This too shall pass,' says the woman to herself after a few moments of agony. 'Yes. It shall pass. It must.'

She is lying prone again on the floor, and gazing at it with dead fish eyes. A thin strand of saliva drools from her mouth and drops to the ground. She traces the drool with the pinkie of her right hand. She pulls the drop of saliva away from her, creating a path like a snail-trail.

'I was a good mother,' she says at last, her voice hoarse

with emotion. 'No one taught me how, but I was, I learnt to be a good mother.' She pauses. 'My baby taught me how. Yes, it was he.'

Her mind eases, she feels her spirit rising. The room with the red oxide floor is visible again. She can see mamma breast feeding Baby Blue, and her gaze is so intense, she can feel the baby's soft gums on her own breast. She feels a kind of ecstasy bubbling inside her. The kind that makes a person weep amid prayer or meditation.

She weeps with abandon, and through the blur of her tears, she re-enters the story, at the exact time when Baby Blue and his family and friends are at the railway station.

It is not easy at first, and the woman thrashes about like a fish caught in a net. A fish with a tremendous zest for life, perhaps because it is a she-fish with its belly full of roe, swimming upstream to release them. She sits up, then throws herself down once more and finally curls up her body. Tight. Knee to heart. The palm of her right hand feels the floor, absorbing the cool indifference of the hard surface. She does not utter it, but Om reverberates, travelling at the speed of sound through the floor, through the dull air in the room, crackling static, as it reignites her mind, zapping her back to the other mother and child.

She wills her mind to visualise them again. This time, differently. She was, she is, a good mother. She will not tolerate a baby's death even in her saddest imaginings. But something is lost, because something is always lost. She knows this. She even knows what will be lost. She sighs in defeat. And then sighs again, like a fighter about to get up. Something is lost, it is true. But everything is never lost, and that too is true.

8

Gublu-mamu and Blue Bottom are so engrossed in their simple game of making the plastic dog jump and wobble that they do not notice the man with a tray hung from a chord round his neck.

The man is wearing a dirty saffron turban on his head. Curls of crimped hair sneak out from underneath his turban. A U-shaped vermilion tattoo adorns his forehead. He has an intent look on his face. He has something to sell and he desperately needs customers. He holds a bell in his left hand so he can attract the attention of the people at the railway station. His wares are placed on the tray that hangs from a chord, reaching almost to his waist.

His wares are the prints of a few deities, besmirched with vermilion and sandal paste. A wilting garland of Hibiscus flowers snakes its way around the framed pictures of the deities. A small incense holder sits at the centre of the tray in front of the main deity. A couple of incense sticks add their beige ash to the growing pile around the holder. A few coins strewn around the tray advertise the deities' need for money.

The man spots Blue playing with his Gublu-mamu. He notices the two ladies talking near them. Hope lights up in his rheumy eyes. He shakes his bell resolutely and strongly.

The game interrupted, Blue looks up. He sees this apparition with a strange thing around his neck. His first instinct is to run straight into Gublu-mamu's arms and clamour to be picked up. The plastic dog is abandoned, stuffed back into uncle's pocket. Gublu-mamu hoists Blue up. Blue clutches Gublu-mamu's shoulders. He stares with round-eyed horror at the man with the turban and tray.

Mamma notices her baby's distress. She breaks off in mid-conversation and almost snatches Blue back from Gublu-mamu's arms. Gublu-mamu stands there, suddenly feeling unsure of himself.

The seller of piety does not realize that he has frightened

the child. He is too desperate to earn his living. He hopes the big man will give him a couple of coins. He hopes the ladies will throw him some. The man shakes his bell playfully before Blue. He tries to make eye contact with both mamma and Gublu-mamu at the same time.

'Thakur,' says Gublu-mamu to Blue, trying to ease the sudden tension. 'Thakur. Say nomo nomo.'

Gublu-mamu folds his hands and dips his head a couple of times to demonstrate. The other man dips his head and grins encouragingly. His eyes dart between Gublu-mamu and Blue. And, then between mamma and Blue. Mamma clutches Blue to her bosom, looking at the man distrustfully. Blue senses mamma's feelings. He looks at the man and his tray with suspicion. His lower lip trembles. He turns towards mamma but curiosity drives him to look at the shabby creature before him.

Baby Blue looks at the framed pictures, incense, and wilting Hibiscus garland. The pictures are flat two-dimensional garish calendar art prints. There is a picture of Shiva and another of Sri Krishna as a baby. There are a couple of other deities whose likenesses he has never seen before. He has seen the first two pictures before, though right now he has no memory of them. They do not speak to him either. They do not shimmer like they used to before. They are dead pictures. Blue looks at mamma again, and this time he has a question in his eyes.

'Thakur,' says Gublu-mamu again, as he fishes out a few coins for the seller of piety. 'Nomo Nomo.'

'Thakur,' says mamma encouragingly. 'Don't be frightened, darling. That is a God, 'Thakur.' Nomo Nomo. Mamma does Nomo Nomo?' She presses the palms of her hands together.

'Taku,' says Blue, copying mamma. 'Nomo. Nomo.'

He looks at the other man triumphantly. He has said two new words. The words mean nothing. Nor do the pictures on the man's tray. They are not real like mamma, baba, and Gublu-mamu. The yonder does not beckon through the pictures, not anymore. Earthly things now contain wonder for Blue. Still, there is something fascinating about these illusions.

He rolls the words with his little tongue and blows them out with his soft baby lips. 'Taku. Nomo. Nomo.'

Mamma kisses the top of Blue's head, making a mental note to announce this latest addition to his vocabulary to everybody in the family.

Gublu-mamu beams at Blue. 'Clever boy!' He says and caresses Blue's cheeks.

Blue is pleased with himself. He understands that both mamma and Gublu-mamu are proud of him. The words and the pictures of Gods slip into a compartment in his head, like a letter in a mailbox. Later he will be able to connect the two and repeat the words whenever he sees similar pictures and images. And, mamma will be proud of him all over again.

Blue watches, cradled in mamma's arms as the seller of piety turns away from them and starts to thread his way through the crowds, prospecting for more coins, taking his holy pictures with him. The seller of piety has no more interest in them now that he has received payment.

Blue does not know the Gods displayed are nothing more than puppets made for business and entertainment. He would not care if he did. The voice no longer exists for him. The haze has lifted from his eyes. He is here now, in the material world. His transition from spirit to flesh is complete.

The woman laughs. The vision of the seller of piety reminds her how ridiculous people are in their eagerness to appease the Gods, any God. You can slather some vermillion on a stone and the very next moment a crowd will gather to offer fruit and flowers and money. As if God can be bought. She remembers how far she has moved away from all kinds of rituals of piety, she has not even retained the altar dedicated to deities in her home anymore. She no longer sits before brass and clay idols after her bath in the mornings or goes to any temple anymore. She no longer lights lamps in the evenings. She does not celebrate any religious festival. Her house remains dark during Diwali. Only those who know her intimately, know she mutters a certain prayer when she thinks no one is looking.

The woman fears dusk. Her fear is based on both traditional beliefs and the feeling of immense solitude that twilight brings with it. Laying herself down on the floor in the late afternoon has become a habit. She does not remember when she changed her position on the floor or when the floor itself changed. A moment is a treacherous eye-blink. Entire constellations can change the course of their directions in that time. But this is nothing as dramatic as that. Except that the moment has passed. Time has rolled out like a forgotten marble from under the bed. Time no longer holds the same meaning, because she and the world have changed so much since that seeming moment, all those earth-years ago.

9

Time has revolted. Its face has changed, making it another entity altogether. Forty-three years have passed since her private meltdown after reading about the Babri Masjid's demolition. Forty -three years since she had read it for the second time, and a month after it was over. Time has been marching with the clock and the calendar. Time has been naming the hours, days, weeks, months, and years. But to her, it is as if Time has suddenly awakened now.

The woman is alert to the fact that the year according to the calendar is 2035. Alert and terrified. When and how did so much of her life vanish so quickly? Everything has turned strange and distant. In an instant. In an eye-blink.

So much has happened within that span of time. So many things occurred that led to unalterable changes, in people, cultures, societies, and nations. A sly disease was born in that time, feeding on humans. Growing fat, and changing itself several times to fight the vaccines, until human DNA itself mutated, just a tiny bit to accommodate the mutations. That had begun around sixteen years ago. Nothing remained the same afterwards. Perhaps, unbeknownst to mankind, the human species had gone extinct or was in the process of becoming extinct, while a newer type of hominid had emerged or was in the process of emerging amongst them. Just like the Denisovans who had lived and mated with the Neanderthals, and then disappeared.

The woman looks at her hands. She touches her cheeks, as if to find some visible change in herself that would inform her of her changed DNA, and not only the signs of age. Her imaginings have always been freehold. She is untethered by scientific logic and probabilities. It is still exciting for her to imagine herself as a different version of her previous self. She wonders if the one who moves the universe has a hand in it. Or is it by pure natural selection - Nature's non-sentient progress.

The thoughts dart about her mind like minnows in shallow water. Evening gathers around her. A shadow falls and something else grips her — her worry for her son.

She is worried for two reasons.

Her son, a man now, and no longer in his youth's prime, is far away from her. His life is a mystery to her, for the distance is not merely physical. His news reaches her like the scattered leaves of autumn. They crumble in her hands when she tries to scrutinise them. And now, he is at the zone of war. And this is the first reason for her worry.

The war. The war. The war.

The war has mushroomed out of dank soil into fetid air. Its cap nods at a distant pale sun in glee. Its stem clings to earth, where its brethren sleep. They are all rooted together below, like conniving hands clasped under the table, their filaments shooting across countries, unseen by human eyes, until they erupt in some place, shocking their human bystanders, literally knocking them off their feet. The noxious network of war pushing up their snouts to scout for fresh quarry.

The many faces of war erupt in some pockets, pockmark strips of land squashed between sea and hostility. In other places it spreads like a rash. War is besieging earth in all the glory of its angry colours, farther north and farther west of India, yet horribly close to home. It has grown faster and more uncontrolled than the most virulent of weeds. War is a presence now, like a summer fire in a world stacked high with dry timber. The sprouting wars have converged into the third world war. It has become the war the entire world has always dreaded but did not take the steps necessary to avoid. It is the war prophesied centuries ago. The war that countries around the world allowed themselves to be sucked into by participating in petty quarrels in order to prevent it. This war is turning earth into a wasteland.

Do wars really start and end? The woman is doubtful. She is suspicious about the very idea of war. She believes it to be a continuous presence in human life. To her it is a single entity, yes, it is a creature both alive and vicious, and one that possesses the ability to change its face with the expertise of the bohuroopee. The continuous war has fooled people into thinking that it died in one place, and then sprang up again elsewhere.

There really has been one single war uniting the entire world. A war that humans have been consuming with gusto for breakfast, lunch and dinner, and tea and snacks in between. Each time humans became a bit more technologically advanced, more creative. Inventing new names for the same ongoing thing, providing it with new ornaments of weapons, each new version a more vicious improvement on the previous.

Drones have been doing the dirty job for decades now, with increasing sophistication. Drones with the capability of slipping into erstwhile peaceful and happy places and creating havoc, bringing tragedy. Humans have been deployed to help the wounded and the bereaved. To build more drones with the help of other machines. Drones can destroy and kill and maim, but they cannot cure or bring succour. Drones must be programmed by humans. But the number of humans has diminished and continues to do so, day by day.

Her son has left, with his own family, to help the humans or to programme the drones, like all the other sons and daughters of a bewildered generation. They did not start this third world war or The Grand Continuous War, as she likes to call it. The GCW's newest chapter began in earnest thirteen years ago, when Russia declared war against Ukraine, escalating it from its previous plodding progress into a carnage that everyone hoped would be contained within that zone. But it didn't. The world reeled in voyeuristic agony over Ukraine. Many smaller skirmishes were ignored. Until Hamas turned a music festival into a carnage, and the voyeurs teetered as they watched. Hatred's roots lay bleaching under the sun, but so tangled up that no one could tell where it began and where it was going. The war kept on escalating, crackling through air, sizzling through water, crashing through land. A web of unrest spinning their networks of negative impulses. Racing towards the annihilation of civilisation.

In less time than it takes to manufacture a holocaustic weapon, the GCW had engulfed the world. Even those countries wearing placards of peace on their faces have become involved, more directly than they care to admit. No, her son and all the other children of the world did not start this chapter in humanity's history, but it is their lot to fight it. It is their job to find a way to end it or at least contain it, so the rest of the world can believe it is dead and gone, and live in a fool's idea of peace for some time.

A fool's paradise, if there ever was a truer cliché, it was this — the way she had been living almost her entire life. Her own garden of Eden of blissful ignorance. Her home and hearth. Her status as wife. As domestic Goddess. As a mother... Where did it lead, ultimately?

The woman passes the dining hall on her way to the balcony. The dining table is expensive and ugly with sophistication, not something her younger self would have chosen. It is no different from the house they live in now. A high-end condo in an uber secure gated-community. The airspace above it is sheathed by stealth-tech bots that prevent any sign of habitat from leaking skywards. Any sign that would make them a target for any enemy drone that has managed to escape the Indian watchdog drones. Inside the community, they do not have to paper over their windows and lower the volumes of their music systems. They can party safely, though few do, the young being away. Neither sound nor light escapes the invisible cyber security-dome.

Some shanties have sprung up around the perimeter of this community, like elsewhere. Smart minded poor people have figured out that they stand a better chance at survival if they live under the security shadow of the rich. Some members of the condo-community have tried, unsuccessfully, to remove the squatters. But they provide services that many still need from fellow humans, that robots and smart gadgets cannot deliver. What nobody admits is that the biggest benefit is seeing a real human face in proximity, though the disgruntled purists keep trying to keep their space exclusive and pristine. This is another war, which is possibly the mother of all wars, and the reason why humans have been warring down the ages. The war between the haves and the have-nots, the needy and the greedy, the wanting and the wanted.

Nobody speaks about being alone or bereft. Not anymore. Even though there is not a home in the world that does not cocoon a grieving or a frightened parent. The world is in a state of limbo. Everyone lives in fear and hope. Everything is rationed. Except time. When evening comes, time begins to look like a demon.

The second reason, the other thing that is eating up the woman's anguished mind, is that she cannot remember her son's face. His adult face, the way he looks after shedding childhood. In her mind, her most vivid images are of him as a baby. She remembers with crystal clear clarity every detail of his life as a baby, a toddler, and as a very small child. Still chubby and dimpled, with an oversized water bottle hanging from his neck, and school uniform a size too large, because she expects him to grow faster than the school year can move. This is the most grown-up image of him that she can conjure up. After that the memories grow steadily hazier, blanking out from her mind by the time he reaches manhood.

She cannot name the time he left home for good. She calls him always by the endearment she used when he sat in a pram and stared at her with large eyes fringed with long lashes. Perhaps because she was much more physically involved with him when he was small. Perhaps because everything about him, and her experience of him was pure and unblemished. He was incapable of any kind of wickedness or meanness. He was so removed then from the harsh broken voice of youth, and later the stubbly cheeks of adulthood.

She knows this is wrong. Everything is wrong these days. There is no peace anywhere, except in the way the kettle still sings to announce that it is time for tea.

The woman shakes her legs lightly to loosen her arthritic knees. Her stylishly coiffed hair is dishevelled. It looks like a frizzy mass of grey synthetic fibres. Synthetic. She mulls on the word. Everything about human society is just that. How often in her own life has she felt like a plastic doll with arms and legs that moved? How often has she looked at the men around her, including her own husband, and thought of them as automatons? The need to cut through that synthetic casing and reach for the human within, that being of hurtable flesh and blood has caused her more pain. But she has never ignored that need. In her youth, she smeared the unguent of her imagination on her days, and made her life come alive. Her lived imaginings had made her sane when she faced the physical world around her. She should not be bitter now.

She turns towards the window, where her face receives the sun's last ray through the fortified glass panes. The ray is like a heavenly finger beckoning her. She looks away. She calls on a frail hope that quarter of a century will pass, and everything that is happening now will be over for good, and that she will be turned to ash, which in its turn will be fed to earth, and her son will be an old man with grandchildren clambering up his knees. She looks away for a moment, but the sun's ray remains faithful, even as it is dying. The sunray still caresses her face. Time has not moved at all. Not now. Not for her. How sly time is!

The words of a poem splash into her mind, like a spritz of spring water on her face — 'The Malarkey' by Helen Dunmore, a poet and novelist whose book she had won in a social media quiz that she had taken during the pandemic. Those two years of Covid-19, when people were scared witless, and stayed indoors, and sought entertainment and companionship through the electronic media. Cell-phones had turned into lifelines, and computers into islands containing paradise. (She had by then learned to use with confidence, these tools of modern India, which did not exist when her son was a baby.) She had participated in the quiz during a particularly dull evening, having decided to put her mind to good use with a few clever turns of phrases. When her prize came home at long last, she sanitized the outer cover, and sunned the book. After that she did not know what to do with it.

Poetry had never been her thing. Nevertheless, she opened it one day, and read the titular poem, and then, because that poem stayed inside her, she read the others. She returned to 'The Malarkey' again and again, until she could recite it almost in its entirety. Now she tries to dredge up the lines in her mind. The book was lost a long time ago, during one of their endless moves, their constant re-settlings into one life after the next of greater prosperity. For India had begun to leap up the international ladder of success, had become a country gleaming with glory, albeit in a crumbling, eaten-away earth. But the lines elude her now. The poem hovers just out of reach, dropping the images and the meanings of its words into her mind like fishing lines with luscious baits.

Had she read Helen Dunmore as a young woman, the time when she used to stay home with her infant son, in that non-descript town-city, the poet would have certainly visited her, as she went about her household chores, and laid the table for her solitary lunch, after having packed a lunchbox for her husband to take to office earlier in the day. She and Helen Dunmore would have had many pleasant conversations about poetry and fiction and other intellectual things, before sitting down to lunch. Helen would have eaten the fish curry and rice with her fingers from the steel plate, and smiled and spoken about many things other than poetry, as she balanced her posture against the wobbly make-shift dining table. For she was a woman too, wasn't she? Helen would have understood. She would have enriched her in the way only a woman who is also a writer can, by coaxing her with words, the inchoate engagement with books of her younger self. Which in turn would have led to more conversations and tea and meals at her dining table. But that magic had not happened.

By the time the woman heard of Helen Dunmore, and read her book of poems, she had changed as a person. She had become harder and more resilient and blasé, a sophisticate. She no longer lived inside her head. She had learnt to use her tongue like artillery. She was gaunt and beautiful, and her husband was secretly in love with her all over again. He did not know that she saw beyond him because there was nothing in him for her to seek. She had become far removed from their life of shared comforts, and dealt with it like the whores who detach their souls when they serve their customers. They cannot be demeaned further, because their bodies are not sentient during the act, but automatons, and they themselves are far away.

Her son had grown by then, and no longer filled her days the way he used to. She threw successful kitty parties, even as she held her friends at arm's length. She no longer acknowledged the innocent pastimes of her youth. She considered those solitary excursions into imagined glory and intellectual smorgasbords to be the silly extravagances of a naïve young woman. A silly goody-goody fool! That episode of her life embarrassed her. It was her loneliness, she told herself, a most humiliating thing to harbour in one's mind. It had turned her into a diffident woman with an overactive imagination, having conversations with non-existent celebrities. She is relieved no one ever found out. How they would have laughed. And the thought makes her angry.

She is a better person now, she concludes. She is stronger. She no longer feels lonely. She is harder. So hard that her memory has turned dry. Now even the word malarkey rolls around her tongue like a seed one sucks on in the hope that it will magically bring back the fruit already consumed.

'Mmmmalarkey,' she mutters. 'Mmmalarkey...'

The poem unrolls in the dark air before her, like a kineograph. Her mind reworks the images and creates her own version of the poem:

Had she been a good mother? How does her son remember her? She shivers. Why had his mischief not led her back to tenderness?

She peers at the pages flipping fast before her. She tries to push the many little memories dimming the one true picture she wants, but which is wanting.

Her table groans. She used to seat them all, he and his mates, and watch them eat. The misty ghosts of their quick breaths now trail the walls.

The corridors of her home do not resound anymore. At dusk

there is no thump of ball returning, no careless foot fall. The lamp on the study table stays unlit.

She used to cook his favourite dishes, always. But the rising steam had clouded her vision. When had his palate changed?

Dishcloth in hand she had frowned as she leaned against the kitchen counter. Just once, she had turned. When she looked up, the house was filled with deathly silence.

Her insistence on hygiene and routine has grown and grown. And now she has a sparkling home cradling her in its grim sobriety. She feels the pull. Is that a lost ghost or a forsaken memory slinking away?

She shakes herself from the reverie, and tries again.

'Mmmalarkey... Mmmmmalar...'

Her heart feels like a clod that is too dry to coddle a seedling. When do children forsake their parents? When had she forsaken hers? She cannot remember.

Her lips buzz with the suppressed sound.

'Mmmmmm...'

It is a half-born sound. It is not Om. It is Om suppressed.

'When you suppress Om, you end up with malarkey,' says a non-voice. It speaks to her from inside her head. 'Malarkey is part of this whole rigmarole. An enactment. Its purpose is to trap you.'

Entrapment. Life is an entrapment in that case. She shivers again.

Whose hand is at play here? Why has the world been allowed to be the way it is? How much can she question? How much does she comprehend? The questions fly around her like bugs after rainfall in moist air.

The weight of it pushes her down. She sits on a cold stone seat facing her small terrace garden. The stars are feeble in the gloaming. But they manage to instil some joy in her. She gazes up. It is quiet. Still. Peaceful. The universe is so wonderful. She visualises the baby of her imaginings playing hide and seek among the stars.

There are so many worlds out there. As beautiful as this one, yet different. Parallel universes. Each unique. There is beauty everywhere. All you need are the eyes to see it. The destruction of this beautiful world of ours is a temporary mirage. The trick is not to let it fool you. Not to let it draw you in and forget the real world out there. These are the thoughts visiting her now. Quelling the fear pumping through her blood.

She stares at the sky and the trees below it. The dark shapes of homing birds. White flowers opening their petals to greet the night. Passing clouds form a shape in the darkening sky. The woman looks up and sees another woman there. A young woman with faith in her heart, and a smile on her face. The clouds dissipate. A slow shift of light and air. The image dissolves. Lines of smoke drawn by an invisible and eccentric artist. Silence descends like a celestial feather. She feels forgiven. She feels released. She breathes in a long breath.

'Om,' she says at last, expelling the word through her lips and her senses. 'Om,' she repeats. 'OM!' And then the word grips her, and she raises her voice to the firmament. The word gathers up the particles of sound and becomes more words, and then they become much more than words. The old prayer, the *Gayatri Mantra*, she had renounced long ago returns. Her body begins to vibrate with the universe.

She comprehends. She understands. She now knows. This world is nothing but a dream populated by dreamers. Her soul latches on to the truth, suckling on its nourishment. The beauty of the truth shines in the only true words known to her.

The words that are now coursing through her veins and arteries:

Om Bhur bhuvah-swaha
Tat-savitur-varennyam
Bhargo devasya dheemahi
Dhiyo yonah prachodayaat.

Incepta

Afterword

It is a standard practice, something all authors do in their foreword or afterword. Authors thank the editors for their help and involvement. In this case, I am not sure I can. 'Thank You' is simply not enough. This book, *The Woman on the Red Oxide Floor* would not have existed if it hadn't been for my editor, Sucharita Dutta-Asane. It was Sucharita's keen eye that spotted the real story and the real protagonist when the manuscript was an inchoate mass of chapters. It was she who pointed out the way, and held my hand all along. A gifted writer herself, Sucharita brought her writerly sensibilities over to nurture and nourish my manuscript, and turn it into the book that it is today.

I want to thank Dibyajyoti Sarma for his faith in me, to let my novella become a part of the Red River stable. Dibya is patient and sensitive, something I learnt when he published my poetry book, *After Grief*. Books in Dibya's hands turn into works of art. Making them more than the sum of texts and book covers.

My sincerest thanks to Shashi Deshpande, Sukrita Paul Kumar, Samit Basu and Michael J DeLuca, accomplished and established writers and editors, who took the time and the trouble to read *The Woman on the Red Oxide Floor* before its publication, and who believed in it enough to endorse it. I am so grateful to you. Thank you sincerely for your support.

I would be amiss if I did not thank my children, especially my son, who being the first born, literally taught me how to be a mother, showed me what it means to love like a mother. My daughter picked up after him, and whittled down any rough edges left. I thank them both for the gift of their births and the childhoods I got to spend with them, and of course, their unconditional love. Last but not the least, my appreciation of my husband. It is not easy to live with a perennially cranky woman, careless of the practical world around her. Thank you, husband, for your love and patience. I must also mention Lady Highbury, our rumbunctious Shepsky, who fills up our lives with such sweet innocence that it is impossible not to believe the world is a good place after all.

Where a book goes and for how long, who is to tell? Every book has its own life to live and its own readers to propel it forward. All I can say is writing *The Woman on the Red Oxide Floor* has been a wonderful and enriching experience, with credit of course going to Sucharita Dutta-Asane and Dibyajyoti Sarma for making it happen. I hope, for Sucharita's sake and for RED RIVER *Story*'s sake, this little book, this novella of ideas, finds the kind of readership that will nurture dialogues. I hope *The Woman on the Red Oxide Floor* will dock at many reading ports, and that readers will find it meaningful.

Limited edition fiction titles from Red River